The Cusp of Sad

The Cusp of Sad

By Nikki Pison

Little Heart Press
Rosendale, NEW YORK

 Published in the United States by Little Heart Press, Rosendale, New York.

ISBN 978-0-9892459-9-9

Cover artwork: *Chasing the Golden Ball*. Mixed media on canvas. Copyright © 2013 Nikki Pison

Inside artwork:

The Hermit. Mixed media. Copyright © 2013 Nikki Pison
Urban Butterfly. Mixed media. Copyright © 2013 Nikki Pison
Drying Her Wings. Mixed media. Copyright © 2013 Nikki Pison
Chasing the Golden Ball. Mixed media on canvas. Copyright © 2013 Nikki Pison

This is a work of fiction that has been filtered through the imperfect lens of memory and the distortions of fantasy. The resulting mythology may at times resemble the truth.

Even though the events are entirely fictional, the names of factual places and people have been changed to protect the innocent...and the guilty.

This book is dedicated to the memory of
Gale McGovern:

Activist... writer... friend.

Part I:

November 5 – 6, 1988

Chapter 1: The Dress

Sadie Lane

Sadie's combat boots undulated beneath the fraying edges of her wedding dress. She kept her eyes on her feet because that helped her unwilling body move forward. A wet snow had fallen in the night. The resulting slush soaked into her boots and weighed down the bottom third of her dress, which snailed out behind her in thin ribbons of tattered lace. She tried not to look up the street because that made it seem so much further.

Only one more block up Market Street would take her to Ella's door and to a refuge from her foggy mind and numb body. She was terrified of the gaps in her memory of the night before. Vague flashes of making out with a blonde woman in the bathroom stall of the bar churned her stomach. She had woken up on the couch of an apartment she did not recognize. Despite her disorientation, she was relieved to find herself fully clothed.

The dress had been a gag. Halloween had been earlier in the week, and feeling impulsive, Sadie decided to wear the old wedding gown she had stuffed into a $2 bag at a church rummage sale. She created a stir when she came in to the bar. Her friends laughed at the inherent joke of Sadie in a wedding dress. Old drunks asked her where her husband was and hit on her when they found out she was single. The Public was a dive almost exclusively visited by locals. Security at the "Pub" was lax since few college students ventured into its seedy interior. Some of the older looking punks could get away with drinking there. Sadie was only eighteen, but nobody gave her a problem at the Pub.

She cashed her paycheck from working at the deli all week at the bar. Although she promised herself she would only spend $10, she passed a lot of it back to the bartender. She played a game of pool with some older bikers, who bought her shots of tequila to celebrate her non-wedding, and then it got blurry. Sadie remembered being in the bathroom, looking in the mirror and not feeling the usual self-loathing. She admired the contrast of the white dress and pale skin with her black hair and dark kohl around her eyes. Her hair was short in back and stuck up in chaotic and spikey tangles in the front that fell down over one eye, a la Robert Smith.

A woman in her late twenties in tight acid washed jeans came out of the stall. She began oohing over the dress, asking Sadie questions about it, playing with her hair, and telling her how beautiful she was. Flash to kissing and groping in the bathroom stall, feeling slender arms and fingers running over her body and eager gentle lips, while other ladies coming in to use the restroom tried to ignore the giggles and gasping from under the stall door. Sadie remembered the woman, Lisa, introducing her to her boyfriend at the bar, some more drinking with Lisa whispering conspiratorially to her boyfriend in between touching Sadie as much as possible, laughing and stroking her bare arm. Lisa's boyfriend was a jock wearing, no kidding, a pink polo shirt, who kept looking Sadie up and down. The worst thing was that Sadie did not really know what happened next. The bar got noisier and more crowded, and Sadie's memory got more confused. She remembered some of her friends dragging her to the back to play darts, Lisa coming to say good-bye while her boyfriend tried to pull her the opposite direction toward the door, some more pitchers, and then... nothing.

Dim light filtered in through thick ugly curtains when she first opened her eyes. She staggered off the couch and saw too late the bodies on the floor as she tripped over them. Somebody groaned from the impact and she jolted forward, catching herself on the wall. She made it toward a hallway and gratefully found the bathroom. Cupping her hands, she gulped down mouthfuls of lukewarm water to quench the awful parched feeling that invaded her whole body. Immediately she felt the water come back up and found herself retching, sitting on a dirty floor and holding the edges of a grimy toilet. Afterward, she went back out and recognized the shapes on the floor. Two shaved heads, one light and one dark, revealed themselves as Jack and Ditto, the pair of skaters who were inseparable fixtures on the street. They were notorious hangers-on, ending up anywhere they were permitted.

Sadie still couldn't figure out where she was, but seeing Jack and Ditto, she realized she could not have gone far. In the wan light, she found her leather jacket on the floor and stumbled down a stairwell to a door at the bottom leading outside. In the stark daylight, she gathered that she was actually behind the Public. She felt immeasurable relief realizing she had only made it upstairs. Getting her bearings, she knew exactly where she needed to go: Ella's house. Sadie had faith that smoking some of Ella's amazing weed would be the answer to dissolving the gelatinous film that was enveloping her brain. She felt desperate to dispel the wretched embalming fluid that seemed to ooze from her pores and that dark, guilty bundle in the pit of her stomach.

Her journey of two blocks felt like an eternity, but finally she reached the pizza place on the corner that boldly proclaimed it was "Gourmet." She went up the alley past lines of dumpsters and behind the building to knock at the door to #68A. She heard Ella's dog, Kelpie, bark her distinctive high-pitched yelp, and a moment later Ella opened the door to the sight of Sadie, disheveled, reeking of booze, in a wedding dress soaked half way up with mud.

"Don't you look lovely," said Ella.

♦ ♦ ♦

Ella made Sadie wait in the long hallway until she brought out some dry clothes. "Put these on... unless you want to keep wearing that?" she gestured at the sopping dress, making a gray puddle on the linoleum. Ella handed her the stack of clothes and stood waiting. Sadie realized that Ella meant for her to undress right there in the hallway and paused, hoping she would turn away, but Ella just stood there with her hands on her hips. Sadie slowly hung her jacket on a hook and set down the clothes, feeling Ella's eyes on her. She struggled to pull the stiff lace over her shoulders and Ella stepped in to unzip the back before disappearing down the hall. Sadie took advantage of Ella's absence to kick off the rest of the dress, which got tangled up in her boots. She unlaced these quickly and pulled on the dry clothes before Ella reappeared with a big black trash bag for the discarded garment.

Ella's kitchen table was green Formica with little pink triangular shapes weaving through irregular silver lines. Sadie examined it as Ella put a kettle on the stove. "I was hoping you could front me a bag until Friday," she said. "I had money last night, but I guess I lost it at the Pub."

"Sure, no problem," said Ella pushing her long

hair behind her ear as she moved gracefully around the kitchen, opening cabinets, pulling down mismatched cups and a teapot. She tossed an eighth and some rolling papers onto the table in front of Sadie. "Why don't you roll one now for us... for breakfast," Ella said with a smirk before turning back to the stove. Sadie was a bit dazed, and wondered where Ella had taken the weed from.

She only hesitated a moment before her fingers took up the familiar occupation. She made a perfect "V" in the paper, sprinkling the clumps of dark green bud along the center and expertly rolling and tightening. In a few minutes, Ella set two steaming cups on the table and sat directly across from Sadie, producing a little blue lighter covered with metallic foil. Ella reached over and took the finished joint out of Sadie's hand. lighting it and drawing deeply, then handed it back.

Sadie took a long toke. As she exhaled, she experienced a swirl of lightheadedness and felt the pungent smoke permeate her throat and nostrils. Ella and Sadie passed the joint back and forth. Sadie felt relief swell through her body, the dense fog expanded until she was suspended in a sharp, but detached clarity. She looked down at the cup before her. It was brown with orange and yellow flowers and the steam rising up carried wafts of peppermint to her nose. Every heightened sensation, the smell of the tea, her fingers on the ceramic, carried comfort to Sadie. Even the fabric of Ella's clothes against her skin seemed to lull her into feeling safe and warm.

Sadie only noticed now what Ella had given her to wear. The white satin pajama bottoms had big pink roses on them that reminded her of an English country garden. They were lined on the inside with soft flannel. The well-worn thermal shirt seemed buttery smooth next to her skin. She was not sure how much time passed as she sat, but Ella had snubbed out the joint and put it in front of her next to the bag. She now sat watching Sadie with her knees drawn up and both hands around her own cup. Sadie was aware of Ella's hazel cat eyes piercing the distance between them. She dropped her own gaze to the green and pink Formica. "I kissed a girl last night," Sadie blurted out before she could even acknowledge that the words were coming from her mouth.

"Really?" replied Ella, "How was it?"

"It was nice, I mean… I think it was. I was really drunk," Sadie stumbled, unprepared to explore how it made her feel, and especially unable to explain to Ella the shameful knot in the pit of her stomach. "I'm not gay," she insisted. "I mean, I like men. But it's not like I'm a slut or anything. I've only slept with six guys."

Ella took a sip of her tea and regarded Sadie squirming across from her.

"I just feel kind of weird about it. I mean, I don't even know her and I never would have done something like that if I wasn't drunk."

"Hmmm," said Ella.

"I mean, she was nice and it was kind of nice, but I'm really not into that kind of thing."

"Right, because you like men. Men like Raiche

Cameron."

"Shit, Ella!" Sadie snapped. "That's really low. You know what Raiche did to me... everyone knows."

"Not really, I mean I saw the posters, but I don't know what kinds of things you're into." Ella went on in a neutral tone, "I have no idea if you liked it. Raiche told me you did."

"That asshole! No, I didn't like it! I didn't know he was taking my picture, and I had no idea he'd plaster my ass all over Little Heart!" Sadie's heart was pounding. That Fuck! He had hurt her in more ways than one, and now he was going around telling people she had posed for the picture of her ass in fishnets that he had photocopied and attached with wheat paste to every telephone pole and bulletin board in the town. That kind of campaign was usually reserved for band posters, but occasionally it was used to besmirch a properly deserving whore or man-hater. Sadie had no idea why he had done it to her. She thought he really liked her.

She had definitely liked him. He was so sexy, with his devilish smile, dark hair covering one eye, and he was bold enough to wear both leather pants and eyeliner. The night he played at the Sunshine House, Sadie was smitten. A little brave from the plastic cup filled and re-filled from the keg, Sadie approached him. "You were hot tonight!" she said, swaying a little from the beer and trying to be casual.

"Really?" he smiled sideways at her while he coiled up his guitar cord. She was a few inches taller than him and leaned against the wall, trying to disguise her height advantage and her intoxication.

"Yeah, really," Sadie smiled at him over her cup, draining it.

They had rarely spoken before. He was with the older crowd, who mostly kept to themselves, playing music together and occasionally slumming by dipping into sex or drugs with the younger crowd. Raiche invited her home that night, and she went back the next night, too. She had to work all that week, but was planning to search him out that weekend. That Thursday night, Raiche launched the poster campaign, and it was all anyone was talking about. She never went to find him or confront him. She was too humiliated.

"So what was it like, sleeping with Raiche?" Ella asked. "I've always wondered." Sadie found herself a little relieved and even surprised that Ella didn't know. She knew Ella and Raiche were friends, and Ella had a reputation for sleeping with the older guys in Little Heart. She rarely messed around with the kids.

"It was kind of weird. He may be a little guy, but he's pretty aggressive. The first time kind of scared me, to be honest," Sadie said, remembering. "He wouldn't really kiss me and then without any warning he pulled down my underwear and then kind of pushed me down on my back on his bed. Before I knew what was happening he was rolling on a condom. He pinned my legs up against my chest with his body and started shoving his dick inside me, no foreplay or anything. I couldn't really move. I felt totally trapped and I was starting to panic. But then..."

Ella waited, eyes wide.

"Then it was over." Sadie colored deeply and looked down at her hands.

"Yeah," said Ella knowingly. "Yeah, I've been with a lot of guys Sadie, and most of them are two-second wonders. That can be good for us when they're no good anyway. No wonder you're kissing girls!"

Sadie giggled, aware that Ella was actually being nice. Some of the pressure in her chest from retelling the story started to dissolve with the laugh. Ella was apparently not willing to let the topic go, though. "And the posters?" she asked. "How did you let that happen?"

"It was the next night. I don't know why I went back, but I guess I thought he really liked me. I wore these fishnets with no undies and a little black miniskirt, thinking he'd enjoy that. I was leaned over his bed, looking at some of the comics he was working on. He came up behind me and pulled my skirt up over my waist, and I thought it was going to be another quickie like the night before. All of a sudden I saw a flash behind me. I pulled my skirt down and turned around and he was standing there with his camera. I almost got mad, but he said he just wanted something to whack it to when he was old, so I just laughed it off. I really didn't think anything else about it until my big ass was pasted all over the town."

The sting of that betrayal still festered. She had arrived on Market Street that night and the boys started pointing and saying her full name, "Hi,

Sadie *Lane*. Look, it's Sadie *Lane*," with a long emphasis on her last name. It was odd and annoying, but she ignored it at first. It took her a while to notice the posters, which the boys kept glancing at, apparently making a comparison between the ass on the paper and the one standing before them. There it was in black and white, with a bold headline above: "Sadie: *LAIN*." It was an idiotic play on her last name, but no boy in Little Heart would ever again say her full name without thinking about that poster and the double meaning.

"Yeah," said Ella, "Raiche is not really known for his incredible tact."

"Humph, understatement!" replied Sadie. She had an uncomfortable lump in her throat that she tried to dismiss with a cavalier shake of her head and a swig of peppermint tea.

"You look tired, Sadie," said Ella. "Isn't your house outside of town? How were you going to get home?"

"I don't know, walk I guess. Yeah, I'm beat," she admitted. The weed's euphoric effect was starting to fade and was replaced by a pervasive heaviness through her whole body.

"Come on," Ella said reaching out to pull on Sadie's sleeve. Sadie had to keep herself from instinctively yanking away. "Come lie down on the couch. You can take a nap here."

Sadie was not in much of a condition to argue. She followed Ella to the living room, with its long windows overlooking Market Street and a view of the worn bricks of the building across the way. She sat down on the scratchy orange and brown couch and was reminded of the couch she woke up on that morning. Ella vanished and reappeared with a pillow and a sheet and Sadie stretched out, her weary body grateful to recline.

Ella sat on a stool by the window and said, "Now, let me tell you a bedtime story, Sadie. It's pretty embarrassing, and will make you feel better about your interlude with Raiche."

Sadie nodded, wondering what could possibly make her feel better about that.

"It was this past June, and I didn't have the apartment yet. Nobody knew this, but I was actually homeless. You know my mom moved back to South Carolina last year, right? Well, I was supposed to be living with my sister, Aurora, but she ended up following her boyfriend back to Oregon. I had been crashing with friends, but I had no real place to stay. This mechanic I knew owed me some money, so he gave me a car he was working on because he couldn't pay up. It was a little black 2-door. It was summer, so I moved into the car. I could always find a place to park, up in the mountains or out by the flats.

"Well, I got bored with that pretty quick. It was getting hotter and all the weed was drying up around here- do you remember that? All anybody had was that awful dirt weed. I was getting letters from Aurora telling me about the amazing shit they were growing in Oregon. The whole town was jonesing, and I needed to do something drastic, so I decided to go for a road trip."

Sadie interrupted, "Yeah, I remember hearing that you went out West over the summer. You were gone a while, weren't you?"

"About six weeks." Ella paused, seeming lost in thought.

Sadie waited. Then, getting impatient, she urged, "So, was it great?"

Ella sighed, "It was totally epic, Sadie- I have never felt so in control of my life. I had a business plan for the trip, and I stuck to it."

"What do you mean a business plan?"

"Well, I had to fund the trip, so I needed a plan to make it pay for me," Ella looked slyly at Sadie, "and so I found a way to make it pay."

"How?"

"I used my God-given talents!" Noticing Sadie's puzzled expression she added, "My T & A, Sadie. You know, tits and ass!"

"What do you mean, Ella? Did you... did you prostitute yourself?" Sadie asked this haltingly, afraid to hear Ella's response.

"Not exactly," she said. "I just got creative. See, I have a very appealing look to a certain type of guy. You know, the long hair, big eyes, innocent-looking face, like I should be somebody's old-timey sweetheart. I just played a part. First, I mapped out my trip. I didn't take the major roads, just the back roads through small towns. I made a big circle across the country, heading southwest and then up to Oregon and back in a big arc back to New York. I picked places with names like 'Back Creek' and 'Pine Gorge.' In each town where I stopped, I'd scope out the local people, pop in to the diner, get my fluids checked at the service station.

"Sadie, do you know that in every small town

there's a sweet young guy who has never been anywhere but thirsts for adventure? He's a good boy, raised right, but pretty naïve to the world. I found him in every town I stopped. I could pick him out a mile away. I'd sidle up to him and ask him about the local produce, tell him about my sick granny who I was on my way to see a few states over. I'd let him show me around, linger over the pretty scenery, the county fair, the biggest ball of string or whatever else they had to put them on the map, whatever would justify my sticking around a day or two. We'd inevitably have a romantic night under the stars. With a few exceptions, this would culminate in a two-second interlude, my "first time" of course. I'd say a tearful goodbye the next day, telling him I would never forget him.

"And I didn't. In fact, I was meticulous in the notes I kept and made sure to get every one's address. They were all such wholesome kids. There was one ridiculously sexy 17- year-old cowboy in Texas, he was a little out of the mold I was going for, but boy was he cute. Then there was this farmer boy in Iowa. I met him on the way back. Do you know what they grow in Iowa Sadie?"

"Um... no."

"Corn. Do you know what else they grow in Iowa?"

"No, what?"

"Corn. Do you know what else they grow in Iowa?"

"Let me guess," said Sadie, getting irritable. "Corn?"

"Yep, but seriously, they grow a lot of corn in Iowa," said Ella, obviously amusing herself. "But they also grow soybeans, and really good boys. The one there was really different from the rest. Very studious and well-read, a philosophy major at the local community college, but also helping out on his grandfather's soybean farm. Did you know Iowa is a pretty enlightened place? It's not full of ignorant farmers like you might think. They actually have the highest literacy rate in the country. Did you know that Sadie?"

"How do they find the time, with all the growing of the corn?" Sadie almost growled.

"You're funny! No really, they grow men different there. He was a rare breed. I really was sorry to leave him, and when I told him I would never forget him, I meant it. But I left him like all the rest."

"So, there were a lot? How many did you do this with?" Sadie asked incredulously.

"Eighteen. Nine on the way out, and nine on the way back."

"And they paid you? I'm confused."

"No," said Ella, laughing. "No, they thought I was a sweet young thing just passing through."

"So then what?" Sadie was getting tired, and she felt like Ella was purposely toying with her.

"Well, I got out to Oregon and spent a few weeks with Aurora and her man. He's actually a pretty good farmer himself. I came back with several pounds of pot in the spare tire compartment of my trunk with a promise to send them the money for it. I took my time wandering home, making a few more special friends on the way. I came home and started selling my product, and because it was so dry here, I was able to afford this apartment within a few weeks. When I was settled in, I sat down and wrote a heartfelt letter to each of my beaux, telling him what a wonderful time I had had with him, that I would treasure our time for the rest of my life. Unfortunately, I had just found out that I was pregnant, and would need $350 for an abortion. You see, I was about to start school to become a veterinarian, and although I, of course, don't believe in abortion, there was no way I could have a baby without it completely messing up my sweet little life."

Sadie gawked at Ella. "Holy shit, Ella- did it work?"

"Within a few more weeks, the money was rolling in, some in money orders, bank checks, one check written by a mother who had been informed of the unfortunate circumstances and was willing to help to remedy her son's mistake, one even sent me a bunch of crumpled twenties and singles! I don't know, maybe he took them out from underneath his mattress."

"But what about protection, Ella- I mean, if you convinced them that you had gotten knocked up then you must not have used anything. Are you on the pill? What about diseases? Shit, Ella, what about AIDS?"

"These were good boys, Sadie, very inexperienced. I'm sure I was the first, or one of the first, for most of them. And I wasn't worried about getting pregnant. I take wild carrot seed. It makes the lining of the uterus slippery so nothing can implant.

Women have been using it for centuries."

"And they all sent the money?"

"Well, 16 out of the 18. The cowboy sent me an apologetic letter about a sick horse, but I knew he was a long shot anyway. Even with only sixteen, it was a pretty successful venture- I made $5600 and got to see the country! I was able to pay off my weed debt, and I was doubling my investment by selling what I had bought. It was one hell of a summer job! The farm boy from Iowa was the only one who never responded to the letter. That seemed out of character for him, but I didn't think much about it until a few weeks later." Ella actually looked uncomfortable, and Sadie got the distinct impression she did not want to tell the story anymore, but now she was hooked.

"So what happened a few weeks later?" Sadie nudged.

"Well, I was going on with my life, selling my stash, saving up money to buy more. Then one afternoon there's a knock at the door. I open it and there's this guy I don't recognize standing there. All of a sudden, I realize it's the Farm Boy! He's all scrubbed up and looking nervous as hell. I invite him in, and pour him a cup of coffee, trying to act casual, but totally baffled as to why he's there. He's so nervous he's making me nervous, stuttering and staring at my stomach, so of course then I realize he still thinks I'm pregnant. I turn around to get some sugar and when I turn back around, holy shit, Sadie, he's down on one knee!

"He tells me he knows that we don't know each other well, but that he is willing to take responsibility for the baby, and that I can come and live with him on his grandfather's farm in Iowa. He says that I can go to the community college there and that he'll make sure that having the baby won't get in the way of pursuing my education. He apologizes for not getting me a ring, but he spent everything he had getting to New York to see me. He says he has a pickup truck, and he's hoping to take me back with him that day."

"Holy shit," Sadie echoes.

"Yeah, really. You know, until that moment, I had not felt one ounce of guilt for what I had done. It seemed so harmless up until then. I gave those boys some fantastic memories, and they gave me some hush money to shove their mistake under the rug."

"So, what did you do? What did you tell him?"

"I said, 'Look, Farm Boy.' No, just kidding, his name was actually Adam, I said, 'Look, Adam. I really appreciate you coming all this way and the proposal and everything. It's pretty chivalrous of you, pretty rare these days, I'm sure. But listen, Sweetie, it's not even an issue anymore. I had a miscarriage a few days ago. I was going to write to you and let you know, but I've still been feeling pretty weak.'"

"Aahhh, so he bought it?" Sadie's head was pounding, so she lay back and closed her eyes, still listening.

"Yeah, he bought it. He got up off his knees and said he felt pretty silly, and we ended up laughing about it. I told him since he came all that way that he might as well stay a few days. I really did like him- we had some special moments in Iowa, after all.

"It was a really nice time. I brought him up to the mountains and showed him around. We even went pumpkin picking." Ella trailed off, lost in thought. She was quiet for several minutes and then said, "You know, it's funny, but after those few days, I really did get attached to him. He was not like any of these Little Heart boys, that's for sure. He really grew on me. He was smart, really smart. For someone who had never left Iowa before he was pretty worldly. He knew all these things about other cultures and obscure religious traditions.

"He was a feminist, too, actually even called himself a feminist, and not just to get laid, either! That was pretty impressive. Apparently his mother died when he was really young, but somebody raised him right. It was refreshing, he was just so... exotic. Funny to be calling a farm boy exotic, but I just mean he was so different from the misogynistic bastards we grow around here. But then, that's your type, right, Sadie? ...Sadie?"

Ella looked down to the couch and saw Sadie with her eyes closed, mouth opened, finally getting her much needed rest. Ella chuckled softly and pulled the sheet up over her.

♦ ♦ ♦

Sadie awoke hours later to laughter in the other room. This time she knew where she was. Late afternoon light streamed in through the apartment windows. She sat up and looked into the kitchen to see Ella with a gangly kid with a Mohawk behind her, arms wrapped around her waist. She was giggling and trying to disentangle herself, but he was nibbling her neck and talking into her ear. Sadie recognized him as the fifteen-year-old younger brother of one of the punks from town. It was obvious that Ella was either bored or lowering her standards, since she usually only fooled around with men twice his age. But then, Ella seemed fine with sampling all the variety that men had to offer. Sadie remembered fuzzily the strange story about Ella's cross-country journey.

"Oh, Sadie, you're awake!" exclaimed Ella as she noticed Sadie lurching toward the kitchen, still pretty off-balance despite her rest. "You need to go now, Darien," Ella said to the boy. "Sadie's awake now, and it's time for you to go home."

"I can leave..." Sadie started, but Ella shot her a look, and walked the boy out. He reluctantly departed, still protesting and groping at her as she virtually shoved him out the door.

"Kids," she said to Sadie, shaking her head with a laugh. "Are you feeling better?"

"Uh, yeah," Sadie replied. "I actually do. You know, I can go now if you need privacy."

"No! God, no. I needed to get rid of him. I have a friend coming in from out of town tonight, and Darien is so clingy. He's impossible to get rid of. Believe it or not, though, he's really well hung."

Sadie was not sure how to respond to that. "Yeah, so, your friend is coming, so I'll get out of your way. Thanks a lot for letting me crash here. I really needed the sleep. It was a pretty crazy night last night."

"Sounds like it," said Ella with her characteristic smugness.

"So, thanks for the weed, and the tea, and for..." She was going to say something about Ella's unprecedented kindness, but sensed that Ella would not appreciate sentimentality.

"The entertainment?" Ella suggested.

"Sure," said Sadie. "Thanks for the entertainment." She headed toward the hallway by the door where her boots and jacket were and saw the black bag that held her mutilated wedding dress. "Oh, shit. I forgot I'm wearing your clothes. Can I bring them to you tomorrow?"

"Friday is fine. Don't forget your dress!" said Ella, picking up the garbage bag and handing it to Sadie, who had slipped on her boots and leather jacket.

"Oh, yeah, I'll definitely be needing that." She grabbed the sack and headed out the door. "Later."

"Later. Take care, Sadie," said Ella.

Sadie went down the narrow alley that led to the parking lot in the back of Ella's building and went straight to the row of dumpsters. She lifted the metal lid and without any ceremony, dropped the bag in. She let the lid fall with a thunk and kept walking.

Chapter 2: The Tower

Ella Orlando

Ella stood by the sink, washing out her teapot. She looked out the kitchen window, and with satisfaction saw the tower perfectly framed. This particular view was actually why she had taken this apartment. Only a few people knew that she had lived in the attic beneath that tower for a year. She hadn't planned to live there, but fate had stepped in when she had been at a crossroads in her life. She really had no solid plan after Aurora moved to Oregon and her mother returned to the island where she had given birth to Ella sixteen years earlier. Ella and Aurora's mothers had lived together for four years running a successful herb company when they decided to move back to the small island community.

The Colony was an enclave of single women

and lesbians who came to give birth or help with birthing work on one of the smallest barrier islands off the coast of the Carolinas. No grown men were permitted there; it was a place for women. Many of them, like Ella's mother, stayed on and raised their children on the island, successfully farming and living off of the land, learning about childbirth, and living in partnership with other women. The Colony was said to have been founded by a pair of native women, lovers who rebelled against the patriarchal domination in their tribe. The women were excluded from important ceremonies and were not even allowed to touch the medicinal herb that made the "black drink" used in their most important rites. The two determined to run away in order to take the power of the sacred herb into their own hands and create their own tribe, immune to the cruelty of men.

One of the women was pregnant from a vicious rape that had been inflicted on her as punishment for refusing to marry. Her lover used the sacred herbs to assist in her birth, becoming the first Chief Midwife. This title would be passed on over the following centuries from woman to woman. A network of spies was said to have existed between the women who remained with the tribe and the founders. Those who experienced male brutality often just disappeared into the night. When the European colonists started arriving, this kindness was extended to European women, too, and then later to escaped and then freed slaves. The philosophy was that women were an entirely separate race, and that this fundamental truth was stronger than any cultural or ethnic differences. When a woman found herself in precarious circumstances, she was embraced and sheltered in what later came to be called the Colony.

When Ella's mother came to the island to give birth in 1971, there was an underground web of information about the Colony that had extended across the country from former Colonists or children who had been raised on the island. Women seeking to study midwifery would often come to the island for a few years to help with the births, and then bring their education back to the mainland. Information about the existence of the Colony was passed on with discretion, from woman to woman, as it was needed.

Ella's mother, Mary Ellen, had become involved with a married man. When he discovered she was pregnant, he turned his back on her, refusing to see or acknowledge her. She found out about the Colony from a friend who had given birth there several years earlier, and went there carrying nothing but a small bag of clothes. She was taken in, given chores appropriate to her advancing pregnancy, and in a few months' time, Ella was born. Ella's mother fell in love with the woman who delivered Ella, and they were married the next spring in a ceremony that had evolved on the island.

After her wife was killed in a turbulent storm that swept the island a decade later, Mary Ellen brought Ella back to her home state of New York. Both were grieving, and Mary Ellen was so wrapped up in her own mourning that she did not notice how harsh the transition was for Ella. Given the environment in which Ella had been raised, with no men, two mothers, and surrounded by the power of the Atlantic, nature, and birth, it is no wonder that Ella did not exactly fit in with mainstream American culture. She entered a society that was just discovering shopping malls, and the other kids laughed at Ella's homemade clothes. She also had a strange accent, a dialect from the island that sounded almost Irish. Although she quickly lost the accent and even acquired store-bought clothes, her social isolation was already entrenched.

About a year after Ella came to Little Heart, Aurora moved there from Michigan. She experienced her own alienation, having been born in Columbia and only in the States for a few years, with all the trappings of a "foreigner," including olive skin, accent, and her own subtle differences in dress. Although she was friendly and spoke English fluently, the White girls picked up on her outsider status in a second, and avoided her like the plague. Little Heart was a very White community at the time. It was a long way away from celebrating cultural differences, or even just pretending to, such as would soon become the trend.

Sitting alone on the swings at recess, Ella was so used to being ignored or taunted that she did not look up when Aurora approached. By the time the bell rang, they were best friends, and they stayed that way even after their mothers became lovers and they all moved in together. Aurora's mother was a short, full-figured little woman with radiant skin and gorgeous long hair. With her ready laugh and sweet disposition, it was easy to see why Ella's mother fell for her. Ella fell for her, too, and she quickly replaced the mother she had lost. Aurora was the sister Ella never had, and they were rarely separated. The bullying and ostracism at school stopped when they began to sell weed, and their quality product quickly overtook the high school market.

At the end of their sophomore year in high school, Ella and Aurora announced to their mothers that they were quitting school, getting full-time jobs, and pursuing equivalency diplomas. This was a cover for getting an apartment together to sell weed without having to dance around the obstacle of two over-involved mothers. The same day, their mothers announced to them that they were actually moving back to the island. Mary Ellen had been summoned to replace the Chief Midwife, who had died and named her as heir on her deathbed. They were intending for the girls to go with them, but with two headstrong young women, they soon realized it was easier to agree to let them stay and get an apartment together. They trusted in their daughters' relationship and that they would never let harm come to one another. They were packed up and gone the next week.

Their moms had no way to know that within a month Aurora would decide to follow her boyfriend, their biggest weed connection, back to Oregon to help him on his pot farm, leaving Ella to fend for herself. They had not gotten an apartment yet, since they were riding out the lease in their mothers' rented house. Ella was not sure what to do. She was making some money from selling, but had to save so much of what she made to buy the next quarter pound that she never seemed to put aside enough for security and first month's rent on a place. It did not occur to Ella to follow Aurora to Oregon, nor did it occur to Aurora to ask her. Both of them seemed to sense that this was the natural separation that was intended for them. They agreed to keep the pretense up of living together to spare their mothers any concern, and from that point on, Ella repackaged letters from Aurora and sent them to the Colony postmarked from Little Heart.

On her first day alone in Little Heart, Ella wandered the streets. She did not really like to muddy her business with emotional entanglements, so she mostly had customers rather than friends. She had never really needed more than Aurora. She was also not interested in staying with one of her lovers, since this also could involve complications. She walked to the river and considered an encampment there, but a light rain helped her to see that camping by the river would bring some serious inconveniences, and it would be difficult to store her product safely. She walked up through the campus of the college and went in to an office building, surveyed a neglected lounge with large cushy couches and considered how she could get in and out of the building while evading security observation. Ella kept this as an alternative in the back of her mind and headed back to town to drop off an eighth with the owner of the deli, a regular.

On her way, she took a shortcut around the back of a sprawling old building on the fringes of campus that until a few years earlier had been an experimental grade school used to train new teachers from the college's education program. Now it was mostly abandoned, with big empty classrooms, some isolated offices, and a small child care center. Ella and Aurora had spent a lot of time inside the vacated building. They mostly hung out in the old gym in the back, killing time when they skipped school together.

As she walked down the narrow alley behind the building a pigeon darted past Ella and up over the eaves toward the old clock tower at the front of the building. The tower had once held a bell, but now was an empty chamber with columns supporting a domed spire. The ivory dome stood out against the metal roof and dark bricks of the building. It seemed lit with a magnificent inner glow, as if it were a living being. The pigeon swooped down, landing on the rim of the tower, then disappeared inside the hollow.

Following an instinct, Ella tried the big metal door at the back of the building and it opened easily. She passed into a stairwell and vaguely followed some inner passageways through an old girls' locker room and down dark hallways lit only by dim fluorescents, sparse windows, and the occasional illuminated exit sign. She found her way to the front of the building and recognized the inside of the main entrance. Ella climbed the central staircase, remembering stories she had heard about a locker on the third floor that was open at the top. Delinquent hippie schoolchildren of years past climbed up the locker to smoke pot in the attic. The attic door was locked, so Ella went back to the third floor landing. It opened up into the middle of a long straight passageway with a big window at either end. Classrooms stood vacant on either side, their doors wide as if waiting for the children to return. Ella's light footsteps bounced off quiet blackboards and disturbed the eerily stilled air. She silently began to open a few of the hundreds of lockers that lined the hall.

Ella was beginning to think that even if there were such a locker, administrators would have long since found it and sealed it up. Then with surprise, she came to #343. The locker door sounded different from the others when she opened it and Ella looked up into the black rectangle that replaced where the top of the locker should have been. Her heart beating, she did some quick calculations in her mind and stepped inside. It was hard, the first time, using her knees and back to wedge herself in and inch her way up inside until she could reach over the top and pull herself up. Her legs thumped the metal and echoed down hollowly, and Ella wondered if there was anyone in the floors below who could hear it. When she was able to push her body over the top, she found herself in a low sub-floor below the attic. Beams ran through insulation, rat droppings, and other refuse.

It was dark, but she was able to walk along the beams to where she could pull herself up into the wide attic. It looked so expansive the first time she saw it, a long giant room with a wood floor and a high open peaked roof with a round window at each end. There were some old desks stacked on one side, and ladders, buckets, and other maintenance items lying around undisturbed, collecting years of attic dust. Ella's heart stopped when she saw the opening to the tower in the middle of the ceiling. Out of the center of the attic floor rose two parallel iron bars only about six inches apart with rungs every foot or so, a spindly little ladder that led to the tower above. Ella did not hesitate. The bars were surprisingly sturdy, and she began her ascent. She was not afraid of heights, but as she climbed ten, then twenty feet in the air on the narrow steps, where only one foot or hand could fit at once, she had a sense of vertigo looking out into the open space of the attic. She clung close to the bars and decided to only look up.

At the top, she found herself in a small chamber face to face with several surprised pigeons. They scolded her and quickly made their escape out of the square hole that led to the domed tower. Ella poked her head out of the top of the tower and the fresh breeze made her realize how stuffy the air in the attic had been, overwhelmed with decades of bird droppings. Pulling herself up to sit on the inner ledge of the tower, eight creamy columns rose up encapsulating her, as if she were the bell that had once been housed there. If she had not been afraid to be noticed, she could have stood up in the tower easily and would not have even been able to reach the domed roof with her arms outstretched.

Looking out, she saw Little Heart in a way she

had never seen it before. The cars on Market Street rolled noiselessly along. The police and fire station nearby seemed like harmless props, and squad cars just toys. Echoed laughter of children from the playground across the street traveled in a disrupted zigzag pattern to her ears, out of sync with the frenetic movements below. She was removed from everything, yet felt closer to the town than she had ever felt. Worrying about being seen, Ella went back inside and made the shaky journey back down the ladder.

She went to deliver her weed, then went to Zep's house. Zep was one of her only real friends besides Aurora. He was thirty-one, an ex-heroin addict and bass player who had gotten sober and remained on the outskirts of Little Heart society. He was included for being a musician, but excluded for not getting high like everyone else. Zep was enough of an outsider to appeal to Ella, and she enjoyed talking to him. He had a deep monotone, speaking without breaking eye contact through almost disinterested drooping eyelids. Many were unsettled by his direct gaze and how he never seemed to change his facial expression or tone of voice. He talked candidly about his sexual exploits, enunciating words like "fucking" with as little emotion as if he were soliloquizing about plant rotation. Ella appreciated Zep's intensity and intellect, and the fact that he never hit on her.

She picked up her sleeping bag and duffle bag of clothes and told Zep where she was going, entirely trusting his ability to keep a secret. "What if you get caught?" Zep wanted to know.

"Nah," said Ella. "Nobody pays any attention to that building, not even campus security. There's nothing there." Ella found that the metal door in the back of the building was almost always unlocked. She left a window cracked at the back for the rare times when someone noticed and locked the door.

"It sounds pretty inconvenient, going up and down a locker," Zep remarked, next time she visited.

"No, man. I found out that I can prop the attic door open. It locks from the inside, but I wedge a piece of cardboard in there when I go out. Then I can just get back in through the door and I don't have to climb up the locker." Since the second and third floors of the building were completely empty, she was even able to use the restrooms on the floor below, or bring up a bucket of water for cleaning or for cooking on the hot plate that Zep had given her.

"You need to make sure nobody sees you," said Zep.

"I'm always careful," said Ella. "I don't even usually go out when it's light." She made sure she was extremely quiet and never came or left in broad daylight. Sometimes she would leave early in the morning and stay out all day, but most days she stayed in, reading books from the library, cleaning, organizing, and hand stitching clothes from the scraps she pulled from the Salvation Army donation dumpster. She loved having the expanse of the attic as her living space, with her bedroll right in the middle, and the tower as her balcony.

After dark she would prop open the attic door so that she wouldn't have to climb up the locker when she returned, and then head to town to deliver her dry goods. She was still small-scale then, but she made enough to buy food, basic necessities, and to re-fill her stash for selling and smoking. When her work, or the occasional visit to Zep, was done for the evening and she had picked up whatever supplies she needed for the next day, she would head home to the attic and to her tower.

"You know, you could stay here some nights if you wanted," Zep reminded her.

"Thanks, Zep," she said, "but I would miss my tower."

The ladder became easy after a few days, and she had no trouble sprinting up or down it, even when she was fairly well lit. She loved the soft coos of the sleeping pigeons, who always shifted and fluttered a little when she went up at night. She loved the coolness of the air when she reached the night sky and sat out in the open, dazzled by the sweet circles of streetlights and sparkle of nightlife in the town that faded into the spattering of stars above. She would roll a joint and take the whole world in through her lungs, feeling more peace than she had ever known. When she was high in the tower, she felt like she was exactly where she belonged, like she had found her place in the heart of the universe.

When the weed dried up at the end of almost a year in the tower, she made her decision to leave for the journey to Oregon. "I can't pass off this dirt weed in good conscience," she complained to Zep, who was always supportive of her business ventures despite being clean himself. "I've built a reputation on having high quality product and this shit is a joke. Aurora says the bounty there is mind-blowing." She had stayed in regular contact with Aurora through a P.O. box that Zep faithfully checked for her.

"Traveling by yourself could be dangerous. The world is full of predators."

"Ha! Zep, don't you know me by now?"

"Ah, yes. Silly me. Nobody is a fiercer predator than you, Ella."

The hardest part was saying goodbye to her attic home. Even though she thought at first that she would return there when she got back, the seclusion and sneaking around at night had taken a toll on her, and she also knew that she would not be able to process the volume of pot that she wanted to turn around living in such conditions. Her last day there was her birthday. She turned seventeen by herself, alone in the tower. She spent her day cleaning the attic, removing any trace that a sixteen-year-old girl had lived there for a year.

♦ ♦ ♦

Ella stood at her kitchen sink with her hands in the warm suds of the dishwater, gazing out the window at the tower. She sighed remembering her time in the attic, how close to everything she felt there, removed from it all.

The knock at the door startled her out of her

reverie, and Kelpie's bark ushered her to welcome in her friend, who had come on his Harley from Philadelphia, where he had lived for the past six months. He had left right after she had gone on her cross-country trip.

"Hey, Moonface," Zep said with a rare smile, striding past her in his leather and chaps. It was his nickname for her, which he claimed was due to her sweet countenance.

"What, no hug?" Ella responded. He put his helmet down on the table and gave her a stiff, but sincere hug.

"That was a brutal ride," said Zep, "but that's life, isn't it, ugly, brutish, and short? How's business?"

"Fine," Ella responded, always amused at Zep's vested interest in her wheeling and dealing.

"Yeah, well, somebody has to keep the masses placated," Zep said flatly, "and you won't find any lack of sheep around here, just waiting for somebody to drug them, tell them what to do, and then take responsibility for them when they do wrong. People are just herd animals, Ella, and all they really want is to follow the herd." He paced around the kitchen, looking into the sink, out the window, then looked at her directly. "But you're different, aren't you?"

"I hope so," laughed Ella.

"Yeah, you're not like the Little Hearted around here, that's for sure." He continued pacing, obviously still wound up from his journey. "Best thing I ever did was move away. So what if I'm living in the ghetto. At least they all know they're animals there. They know they're the dregs of society. It's survival of the fittest, and nobody pretends it's any different. "

"So it's pretty rough there?" Ella asked, wondering how Zep was fitting in to Philly, where he knew no one and had gotten a job as a parking attendant. She still did not really understanding the reasons for his move.

"No, it's refreshing- it's real. I prefer it. Nobody shines you on, pretends to like you and then stabs you in the back, throws you under the bus, feeds on your carcass like the cannibals around here. Everyone in this town is phony. There's nothing authentic here." He went back to the sink and got himself a glass of water, drinking the whole glass down. Finally, he sat down at the kitchen table, leaning back in the chair with his long limbs extended and appraised Ella through droopy eyes. "Except you, Ella. You're the real deal. How many guys are you sleeping with these days?"

"Um... three."

"Excellent," he nodded. "Are you using condoms?"

"Um... no, I mean, I'm still taking the wild carrot seed. That works for me."

"Pregnancy is only one of the reasons to use condoms, Ella," Zep lectured. Others found Zep's directness abrasive. Ella loved it. "There are a lot of diseases out there, especially with all the drug use in this town. Besides, the human body is very tricky. The urge to procreate is built in way down at a molecular level. Any chance it has to sidestep your methods it will. Plus, all women want babies."

"Not me," said Ella indignantly.

"Not consciously, but all women are designed to want to breed and make babies for men, and they will pick the stupidest, but strongest ones to procreate with." He leaned forward, "Men want to breed to possess women, and women want to breed to possess men. It's unavoidable. It's why I got a vasectomy three years ago. I wanted to take that out of the equation. Even women who say they don't want babies freak out when they find out I have a vasectomy. They say they don't want babies, but they really do. It's why they eventually reject and shun me. I can never fulfill their unconscious fantasy of baby-having, so I'm useless to them."

"Maybe they just can't handle your uplifting and positive demeanor," Ella joked.

"Very funny, but I'm not kidding. Women want babies. You can't help it. It's not your fault, but it's the way you can rise above the animals. You choose not to procreate and then you can be something more than a breeding sheep. Your mom's a dyke, so you at least have a shot of escaping that fate. You have the biology, but maybe you haven't been as brainwashed as most women are," He looked at her more intently than usual. "Don't be a victim of your body, Ella. Use the carrot seed, but use a condom every time, too. You need to make sure you don't fall prey to your biology. You're too smart for that. It would be a waste of your intelligence."

"Okay, Zep, I'll use condoms," Ella contended.

"Good."

"You want something to eat? You must be hungry."

"No dairy, no meat, no wheat."

"I have some corn pasta. I knew you were coming so I got it at the health food store. Also, eggplant, do you eat eggplant? And I bought soy cheese, have you ever had that? I'll make a meat-dairy-wheat-free eggplant parmesan."

"I love you," Zep said, in his flat monotone.

"I love you, too," said Ella, and she began to cook.

After dinner, Zep decided to go visit a few of the women who he alternately revered and insisted were shunning him, and Ella had a quiet night at home interrupted only by a few customers dropping by. She had told her boys to stay away for the next few nights, and Ella was grateful that they seemed to be listening. At the end of the quiet evening, Ella left the door unlocked for Zep and went to bed. She smoked a bowl, lit a candle in her room, and crawled into her little cavern. She had dragged a futon into the walk-in closet of her bedroom when she moved in, strung red Christmas lights around the doorway, and hung tapestries on the inside walls so that her bed was like a little cave. She knew that the boys on Market Street called it her "lair," but she didn't care. Kelpie jumped in and snuggled up next to her. She always slept with her dog, and had been known to kick men out of her bed when she was done with them to make room for her canine friend.

She did not know how long she had been sleeping when she heard Zep talking to her.

"Ella, it's burning," he was saying, and at first she thought he was scolding her for leaving on the candle.

"Oh, sorry, fell asleep," she mumbled.

"No, Ella- the tower's burning," he said.

Ella shot up in bed.

"What?"

"Your tower. It's burning," he said.

Ella jumped up and ran to the kitchen window and saw that the tower- *her tower*- was indeed on fire. Flames licked the sky, and Ella realized there were sirens wailing.

"Oh my god, oh my god, oh my god!" Ella was in a frenzy, pulling on her boots over her pajamas and throwing on her leather. "I need to get there."

"I'll come with you," said Zep.

They took the shortcut through the back parking lot, down a side street, and up the incline that led to the large grassy field that faced the old building. When they got to the top, Ella stood there on the edge of the field, with the expanse of black grass between her and her old home. The sky lit up with the flames and the lights shone on the building from the fire trucks. Already, streams of water were being aimed at the tower.

"It's like a nightmare," said Ella. How could the tower be burning? It didn't make any sense. Just the tower, the rest of the building untouched.

She leaned against Zep, who put an arm protectively around her. Tears streamed down her face.

Chapter 3: Tape

Lilli Vaughn

Lilli stumbled out of bed, finally hearing the pounding on the door that she realized had been going on for some time. "I'm coming!" she yelled. She opened the door to see her annoyed older sister holding the hand of her three-year-old son, with an impatient scowl on her face.

"I've been out here for 10 minutes, Lilli! You said you would watch Kairo today, and you know I have to make coffee for the meeting," she pushed past Lilli, dragging her son. "You're so fucking unreliable! Do you know it's after noon? What the hell are you doing still sleeping? What, were you out drinking all night?"

"Not everybody has a problem with alcohol, Finn," Lilli said, annoyed with her sister, and taking her nephew by the hand, "Come on, Ro-Ro. Lilli will hang out with you while Mommy goes to the meeting." Her sister had become so holier-than-thou since quitting everything and starting to go to meetings six months ago. It was pretty irritating.

"Well, I'm really worried about you, Lillian," Finn switched to a concerned tone that sounded condescending to Lilli. "You sleep all day, your boyfriend is almost twice your age, and you really shouldn't even be living by yourself."

"I'm not living by myself, *Finnian*. I live with Hugh. And with four other people... actually five now that Jesse's girlfriend is here all the time."

"You know what I mean. You're sixteen, Lilli. You should be at home with mom. You should be going to school."

"You're such a hypocrite, Finn. You dropped out of school, too."

"Yeah, but I'm going back to school now. And I wish I had never dropped out. It's where I went wrong in my life- when I started really screwing up. It's hard to go back after so many years."

"Yeah, well, not everybody is you, Finn. I don't have a drug problem, or an alcohol problem, and quitting school was the best thing I ever did. I like my life, and I'm having fun, so you should just leave me alone about it," Lilli was tired, and tired of the lecture. Just because Finnian was eight years older didn't mean she needed to give her a hard time about everything. She'd gotten so serious since she got sober. She used to be a lot more fun.

"I'm just concerned about you, Lilli. I see the road you're headed down, and I want to help you to avoid the mistakes I made," Finn sounded remorseful, but Lilli felt like it was contrived and that Finn really enjoyed putting her down.

"Well I don't need any help," Lilli replied. "Come on, Ro, let's go into my room," she turned to her nephew who had knelt down and was petting one of the two little black kittens that had become the house mascots.

"Hi kitty, kitty, kitty, kitty," he was saying under his breath, tuning out the conflict between his mom and Aunt Lilli.

"Okay, I'll be back about 3:30. The meeting is over at 2:00 and I need to clean up and then I'm going to the diner with my sponsor for a little bit, okay? Thanks, Lil," she gave her sister a quick hug and, forgetting to say goodbye to Kairo, went out the door.

"Mommy?" Kairo looked up from petting the cat.

"Mommy will be back in a little bit, Ro. Come on, let's go see Hughey." They went back to Lilli and Hugh's room off the kitchen. Hugh's black curly hair was splayed out on the pillow. Lilli loved the way he looked while he was sleeping and went over to kiss him.

Hugh grumbled, "Cut it out, Lil."

"Look who's here, Hughey. It's Ro-Ro. Finn just dropped him off."

Hugh opened one eye. "Hi, Kairo, howya doin' buddy?" and promptly dropped back to sleep. Lilli was tired, too, and snuggled up next to him. Kairo started looking at things in the room, which was littered with garbage, dirty clothes, and a collection of musical instruments and equipment.

"Don't touch any of Hugh's music stuff, Ro," Lilli warned. Kairo looked at her and smiled. "I'm serious," she said.

She tried to keep talking to Kairo to keep him occupied, but she couldn't resist the warmth of being under the covers with Hugh and the drowsy lull of cars buzzing by in the street below. They had been up late the night before filming a movie that they had worked on with their housemates and some other townies. The film was about aliens that came to rape members of an incestuous backwoods family. It had been hilarious, and they had been working on it all day and into the evening, with Hugh as the overly-serious narrator and Lilli and the other housemates as members of the ignorant, sheep fornicating, sister, brother, and mother-fucking family. That had kept them busy all night until they were pulled away by news of the tower.

After midnight, Jack and Ditto, who had popped out hours earlier to buy a bag of weed from Ella, came running up to the apartment to tell them the news. They all ran to the field to watch it burn and had stayed there far into the night. Hugh had even filmed some of it to integrate it into the plot of the alien invasion. It ended up taking most of the night to edit.

Kairo was stacking up some plastic cups on a hard-backed suitcase, which seemed pretty harmless, so Lilli zoned out, thinking about her man next to her, and how they had fallen in love. She was bouncing around, had been jilted and rejected by various Little Heart delinquents, was sad and depressed, and feeling pretty terrible about herself when she bumped into Hugh on Chapel Street in front of the Sunshine House. She had met him before, hanging out with Raiche and Zep, and he was funny and nice to her. He seemed about a zillion years old, but she was really, really lonely. He said it was his birthday, and surprised, she told him that the next day was her birthday. She was also surprised to learn that he was only turning twenty-eight. She had assumed he was much older, with his large frame and voice raspy from years of smoking Camel straights.

They decided to celebrate, and Hugh went around the corner to buy them a six pack of tall boys. This, Lilli had found, was the benefit of hanging out with older guys- they could buy beer for her. She drank two and he drank four as they sat on the steps of the Sunshine House. Hugh told her about when he had lived there years ago, and his band, the Shines, that had recently gotten reunited since he had moved back into the area several months earlier. Raiche was in Hugh's band, but was on tour with his other band in Europe for at least another month. Lilli was technically, at least she thought, dating Raiche. However, Hugh broke the bad news to Lilli that Raiche had told him he was just screwing her and they weren't together. She was disheartened by this information, having held out hope that they were more than what Raiche apparently thought they were. Lilli started to see that waiting for him was futile.

When Hugh kissed her, she only resisted inside, still clinging to some sense of loyalty to Raiche.

When he went to get more beer, she stopped resisting at all. They ended up in the back seat of Hugh's friend's classic Ford. He said his friend would not mind, and his place was about 30 miles away in Woodvale. He did not have his own car. They had been inseparable since then. At first Lilli was just so painfully lonely that she was settling. It was a completely novel experience for her to have someone doting on her. Pretty soon, it had become a strong attachment, fostered by someone who actually wanted to be with her and plastered together by lovemaking.

She had been with plenty of guys; too many, really. When she slept with random men, she always hoped it would result in one of them responding to her willingness with adoration, but she was generally cheaply rewarded. Each encounter left her feeling worse about herself, and more alone. She was generally just a receptacle for the men she gave herself to. With Hugh, she found that she was actually able to have orgasms, something most of her brief escapades had been lacking.

Her mother was at first alarmed by Hugh's age, but like with most other things, gave way to her daughter's wishes, especially when she realized that he was not going anywhere. They lived with her mom for the first month, then moved into the apartment at 69 Market Street, above the old record store, when a room became available. Lilli was happier than she had ever been. The truth was that she had been hanging on by a thread over the past year, and had only narrowly refrained from killing herself. Ending the pain was an ever-present thought in her mind. When she was spiraling into despair, she would drink, sleep with a random inappropriate partner, and then hate herself even more.

Her best friend, Sasha, was one of the only people who stuck by her, even though she became impatient with Lilli's drunken benders and indiscriminate promiscuity. Lilli rewarded Sasha's loyalty by sleeping with her boyfriend, Sandler, led on by the hope of a reciprocated attachment. This immediately and irreparably destroyed their friendship, of course, and when Sandler moved on from Lilli to pursue Ella a few weeks later, Lilli was left totally alone with the whole town hating her for betraying Sasha.

It was during that time that she had fallen prey to Raiche. She was always a little infatuated with him, and he had played on this for years. Fully aware of her vulnerability, he set up a scenario when she was inebriated where he handcuffed her face down on his bed with a few of his friends there to watch. Lilli tried to protest, but he whispered in her ear, telling her nobody would hurt her. Then he encouraged one of his band-mates, who Lilli barely knew, to have sex with her from behind as she lay in a puddle of her own drool. Lilli was so out of it that she actually thought it was Raiche who had fucked her. When she went to confront him about it the next day, he told her who had really had sex with her. She didn't believe him at first. Later, it was confirmed by other sources until she had to accept that it was true. She did not know how to process the information that this person she never even spoken to had penetrated her while she lay face down, half passed out, with her ass in the air and her hands cuffed behind her.

The rumor mill was already spreading the story of how Lilli had begged to be tied up and fucked by anyone at all. Instead of being outraged, Lilli was deeply shamed. It was not the first time she had ended up getting drunk and having sex with someone that she hadn't intended to. What was the difference? She ended up blaming herself for putting herself in that situation and added it to the ever-growing bank of self-loathing. She began to seriously consider taking her own life. How she made it through that spring and summer was beyond her, since she constantly thought of ways to end it all.

When Raiche approached her toward the end of summer and told her that he wanted to be with her, Lilli put aside her ambivalence about what had happened to her at his hands, and gratefully fell into bed with him. She had always been so intrigued by him, but spending more time with him, she became numb inside. She had always thought he was a creative genius, with his musical talent and comic book art, but his habits were stagnant and she had to admit, boring, and sex with him left a great deal to be desired. He was snorting heroin frequently, insisting that snorting instead of shooting kept him from becoming addicted, but told Lilli that he would never turn her on to it. It was dangerous, he said, and he would not want to hurt her by introducing her to something like that.

One day he presented her with a little black pin

with a green equal sign on it. She was confused, but he told her it represented how they were equal in the relationship. The concept was totally foreign to Lilli, and she could not comprehend what that could possibly mean. She had never felt equal to anyone in her entire life. It kept her hanging on for a little longer, though, and she did not want to kill herself so much when she fixated on Raiche. When he left to go on tour for two months she hoped that he would ask her to come, but he never did. She resolved to wait for him.

Then she hooked up with Hugh. After hearing Hugh's report of how Raiche had been using her and bragging to his friends about stringing her along, she realized what a fool she had been. Despite the rumors, Raiche had taken some serious heat for orchestrating the "rape" of Lilli that prior winter. Getting her to sleep with him and become devoted to him absolved him of any guilt that was associated with him regarding that incident. If he had really been responsible for it and Lilli had not "wanted it" as he insisted she had, than why would she forgive him enough to get involved with him? It didn't really matter to Lilli, because she had internalized the blame for the whole thing anyway, but to the rest of the town, it secured Raiche's innocence. Lilli was just a slut who had gotten what she deserved.

At least Hugh was there to buffer the pain. Lilli was not sure why he liked her, except maybe that he was as lonely as she was. He was older, had bounced around, had little to nothing to show for his adventures, and nobody to love him at an age when that kind of thing might start wearing on a guy. Lilli had actually seduced older men several times with the thought that maybe someone more mature might be ready to return her love, but it had been as unsuccessful as seducing random strangers. She found out that a willing fourteen, fifteen, or sixteen-year old is a temptation that most older men can't resist during an intoxicated evening, but is an embarrassment too dangerous to acknowledge in the light of day.

Hugh was different, though. He was painfully lonely, she could tell by his pressured, ingratiating speech, his intensity, and his immediate attachment to her. For the first time in her life, somebody wanted a connection to her as much as she wanted a connection with somebody. That was appealing enough to her, on the tail end of her singed feelings about Raiche. She threw herself headlong into Hugh, his music and his aspirations. After abandoning the room he had in Woodvale and living with her mom for a month, they got their own apartment. Now, Hugh was the genius she had hoped to find in Raiche. He created entire albums on his own, playing all instruments, drum machine, singing vocals, backup vocals, and weaving it all together on his four-track recording equipment. It was the epitome of solitary production; he had taken all the feelings Lilli had, but had used it to create something. While Lilli had been drowning in her self-hatred, Hugh had produced music from his. It was admirable.

She had not been lying when she told Finn that she was happy with her life now. There was something so satisfying about watching Hugh sleep, waking up with him every day, watching the little hairs on his face grow into stubble over a few days, and then watching him shave them off. He was her entire universe. He also seemed so proud of her, showing her off to his friends, including rubbing it in Raiche's face when he returned from Europe. When they heard Raiche was back in town they went right to the Trash House where he lived. Hugh wanted to be the first one to tell him. He wasted no time. "Lilli and I are an item now," he said abruptly after they settled into Raiche's room.

"Really?" Raiche seemed surprised, and looked from one to the other. Lilli just looked at the floor.

"Yes, really," Hugh responded. "We're in love. We're living together now."

"Cool," said Raiche, nonchalantly. Lilli could not tell if he was really okay with it. Secretly, she had hoped that he had harbored some feelings for her after all. As much as she wished that he was returning from tour with the hope of still being with her, the thought that she might actually be causing him pain sent a little jolt to her heart. Raiche quickly changed the subject to talk about his trip and when they would be practicing again in the new version of their band. That was that. No drama. What a contrast to the scandal that had ensued when she hooked up with Sasha's boyfriend the winter before. Men are just different, Lilli determined.

Living with Hugh was fun, and she felt like they were a team. He was always dreaming up things to keep them occupied when they could not afford to get high, like the night before with the video. They had drawn a dozen "actors" off the cold November streets to take part in their alien rape film project, each playing a different character: an irritable chicken farmer, a cross-dressing matriarch with a beard, a psychologist sent in to treat the children of the family from the residual trauma of being violated by aliens, a priest who counseled them about all the sin involved.

Lilli had gone to the bag sale at the church and had filled two bags with crazy, tacky, outdated clothes, and these had become costumes for the cast. It was a day-long event, and all of their housemates and the street kids had gotten involved. By the time they were done, it was dark and the lights of cars could be seen making their slow crawl down Market Street two floors below. This was the kind of thing that made Lilli really love Hugh. She had been so stuck and frozen in her despair that she could not even write a sentence or pick up a paintbrush. Hugh was so energetic. He tackled each day with a kind of vigor and creativity that pulled her along and into motion. It was literally saving her life. So, she was grateful, too. He was a little high strung and sometimes embarrassed her by talking too much, but she loved him.

♦ ♦ ♦

She had dozed off for quite some time while thinking of the past few months and had completely forgotten about Kairo. He now sat at the end of their bed, a twin mattress on the floor, talking quietly to himself. She bolted up and saw him at the foot of the bed with his back to her. She almost lay back down, but then saw that he was playing with something long, black, and shiny.

"Kairo! What do you have?" she yelled. Kairo turned around with a smile and held up handfuls of iridescent cassette tape. "Oh my god!" she grumbled and jumped over to grab the spaghetti nightmare from his little hands. He did not protest, just looked at her, dazed at having gotten a reaction when she had been ignoring him for the past hour. "Shit, Kairo! This really sucks! Hugh is going to be so mad," she began untangling the several tapes that Kairo had diligently been unwinding, trying to separate them and keep from breaking the fragile narrow strips.

"Lilli!" Kairo said. "Lilli, me hepp Hughey!"

"Yeah, Kairo, you hepping Hughey, you really hepping," she said sarcastically, trying not to take it out on the kid, and realizing that she got what she deserved for zoning out and leaving him unattended. "Come on Ro-Ro- I'll clean this up later. Let's go in the kitchen."

She picked him up and brought him into the next room, where Jesse James (yes, that was his given name) and his girlfriend, Sarah, were snuggled up in the corner at the round kitchen table. They were sharing a bowl of cereal and taking turns feeding each other with one spoon. Sarah was sweet, but she giggled too much, and played at being a brunette version of Marilyn Monroe, twisting her curly hair around one finger and pretending not to understand anything that was said to her. She and Jesse had been an item for a few weeks, and she had become a fixture in the apartment. Lilli didn't really mind, but it kind of upstaged her sweetly evolving romance with Hugh to have these kids pawing at each other and drooling as they stuck their tongues into every available crevice. It was a little sickening.

"Hi guys," Lilli said, plopping Kairo down at the table.

"Hi Lilli!" they sang in unison. Ugh. Sickening. "Oh, who's this little guy?" said Sarah. "He's so cute!"

"This is Kairo, he's my sister's," said Lilli.

"What a doll!" she said, batting her eyes and making kissy faces at him, continuing her habit of sexualizing herself even by stooping to flirt with a three-year-old.

Kairo watched with big eyes as Sarah smiled at him and Jesse fed her a spoonful of cereal.

"Why he feeding her?" Kairo asked Lilli. Good question. She was perfectly capable of feeding herself, Lilli thought.

"Because she's *my* baby," Jesse replied, to which Sarah giggled and began nibbling Jesse's ear.

"Here Ro-Ro, here's some O's. You like O's?"

"No milk, no milk!" Kairo yelled when she put the bowl down in front of him.

"I already put it in, Ro. Just be good and eat it."

"No milk!" he repeated, but when he realized that Lilli was not taking it back, he poked the spoon in and sampled it. Finding it acceptable, he began eating, with one eye on Jesse and Sarah's shenanigans in the corner.

"That was crazy about the tower last night, wasn't it?" asked Jesse.

"Yeah, insane. It was so weird how it was just the tower, not the rest of the building. Did they find out how the fire started?" Lilli wanted to know.

"I read about it in the paper this morning. The fire company is saying it was an electrical fire- from the clock or something," said Sarah, giving herself away. She could, in fact, read.

"That is so weird. Well, it made great footage! Hugh filmed the whole thing and he's putting it into the movie. It's going to be the aliens attacking. That was so fun yesterday! We need to make a sequel!"

"Yeah, that was classic," said Jesse, who had played the crusty old farmer. "It made me want to go be a farmer and plow some hay!" He nuzzled Sarah, who giggled, of course. She had played the farmer's daughter who was sleeping with her father.

"Why he eating her?" Kairo asked Lilli.

"I don't know, Ro. I really don't know."

A little while later, Finn showed up to pick up Kairo.

Hey, how was your meeting?" asked Lilli, not really wanting to know.

"Oh, it was great, all about the third step, turning your will and your life over to God. It's kind of corny, but it is kind of a relief to think that maybe a higher power might be able to solve some of this shit for us, really." She picked up Kairo. "Hi Ro-Ro. How's my baby? Lilli? His diaper is soaked! It's totally gel! Did you even change him?

"Um.... No," Lilli admitted.

"Holy shit, Lil, he's soaking wet! Where's the diaper bag I left you? Oh, shit, here it is right by the door where I left it, of course! Did you even feed him?" she asked as she tossed Kairo onto the couch and began unsnapping his pants.

"I had O's," volunteered Kairo.

"For lunch? You gave him cereal?" She asked incredulously.

"With *milk*," he added.

"What?? You gave him milk? He can't have milk, Lilli, you know that! He's allergic to milk!"

"Oh crap, I forgot," said Lilli.

"Yeah, well, great, that's what I get for leaving him with you." Finn quickly threw a clean diaper on Kairo and snapped him back up expertly, wrapping the old diaper up and sticking the tape to itself to keep it in a little bundle. She handed the heavy bundle to Lilli. "Do you feel that? That's a diaper that needed to be changed two hours ago," she said accusingly.

"How the hell was I supposed to know," she said weakly. "He didn't tell me."

"Yeah, well, when you have kids, I sure hope you don't wait for them to tell you to change them. Bye, Lilli... and thanks for watching Kairo," she said this without any genuine gratitude.

"Bye Aunt Lil!" Kairo called over his mother's shoulder, waving.

"Bye, sorry about the milk...and the diaper," Lilli waved to her nephew, wishing she had known intuitively what to do with him, the way Finnian seemed to. Maybe some women are born knowing how to take care of babies, she thought. But then, she had me to practice on, Lilli remembered. Finn was already eight when Lilli was born, which was probably why she felt so comfortable bossing Lilli around. Lilli had no little ones to practice with until their mom had their surprise sibling, Josey, who was born right before Kairo. Lilli still thought it was gross that Finn and her mom were pregnant at the same time.

When Josey was born, Lilli was already thirteen and on the cusp of becoming a troubled teen. She was never very involved in taking care of Josey. Having babies at the same time had brought her mother and Finn closer together and pushed Lilli to the outside. It had also been part of the reason she had gotten away with so much over the past few years. It's hard to chase after a teenager when you have a toddler to chase, too. It was also why she put up so little resistance when Lilli told her she and Hugh were getting an apartment together. She was probably relieved on some level.

Lilli's father had died when she was little, so she had never really known him. Her mother began to turn his social security check directly over to her when she moved out. She was grateful for this small amount of money. With it, she was able to pay her portion of the rent and have some left over for incidentals. Checking and seeing that Hugh was still crashed out, Lilli decided to walk down to the street to get them coffee with what was left of what she called in her head the "death money." She put on her thin jacket and went down to Market Street.

It was late afternoon and it was Sunday, so Market Street was quiet. There was some buzzing around the Gayfeather Grill, a breakfast and lunch place that was finishing its business for the day. Lilli saw Rosemarie, one of Hugh's ex-girlfriends, smoking and chatting with some of the other townies at the corner of Chapel Street. She envied her, not for her relationship with Hugh, which from his account, was not anything enviable, but for her self-confidence. She was a short woman with thick legs who always wore conservative long skirts. Rosemarie seemed to have no self-consciousness that she did not comply with conventional Barbie aesthetics, the way that Lilli was acutely aware of her own deficiencies. Lilli watched her talking with her friends, tossing her head as if she had a long mane of hair instead of the closely-cropped cut she wore. Her body movements were languid and relaxed, and she seemed to possess not one ounce of insecurity.

Lilli was hard on herself for her own little body. She was short, or as she told herself, *freakishly* short, and convinced that she was grotesquely shaped, with big rounded breasts, a short undefined waist, and big thighs. She tried to hide this reality with her wardrobe of odd-patterned clothes from the seventies that she picked up at garage and rummage sales, cute flowered dresses that she cut off below her butt over fishnets with combat boots. She felt like this did the most to camouflage her physical disadvantages. If she couldn't blend in because of her height and what she imagined was her disfigured body, she would at least stand out for her inventive attire.

She also looked young, despite her prominent bloom. Between being short and her cherubic face, she had the appearance of someone who looked, well, her age- sixteen. She envied Rosemarie mostly for her age, twenty-three. Being older seemed to hold keys to freedom that Lilli desperately craved, like being able to go where she wanted, bars and parties that she imagined were closed to her. Most of all, she craved freedom from the harsh criticism that she inflicted on herself. She wondered if maybe all of the painful introspection, self-deprecation, and uncomfortable feelings of her teen years would wear off as she got older, as they seemed to have for Rosemarie. She held out hope that she could still get taller, blend in more, and that she might some day cease the onslaught of loathing that, despite Hugh's love, she still had for herself.

"Hey, Peep!" She heard her nickname being called and turned to see some of the skaters approaching, boards in tow. For some reason, she didn't mind when the older people in town called her by her nickname, but it annoyed her when the kids followed suit. She thought of herself as separate from them, especially now that she had an older boyfriend. Jack, Ditto, and Carmine came up from Chapel Street, the former two all smiles. Carmine wore his traditional sardonic smirk.

"Hey, guys, what's up?"

"Going up to campus to skate," said Jack. He was the taller of the two, but both he and Ditto, who was never far behind and whose real name nobody seemed to know, wore similar attire, army drab, Converse sneakers, and shaved heads. They had both been straight-edge when they came on the scene a few years earlier, but like most of the kids who ended up hanging out on Market Street, they eventually succumbed to the favorite pastime of all who dwelled there, and were now some of the biggest potheads around.

Carmine was a moody kid that Lilli had known since kindergarten. His mom was a hippie pot dealer from the days of old. Lilli remembered playing "pot store" with Carmine when they were really little, like six or seven, on the playground, before she had any idea what they were really playing at. He knew a little too much, instructed Lilli how to be a good customer, come in and request Jamaican or Indica. He had a rough childhood, and had carried his difficult upbringing into adolescence. No big surprise.

"Gonna check out the tower, too," mumbled Carmine. "I haven't seen it yet."

"That shit burned right up!" Ditto said excitedly. "It was radical!"

"Yeah," said Lilli. "Hugh got the footage. He put it into the movie."

"Awesome! 'It's an alien pod!'" Jack quoted a line from their shoot the day before, and they all cracked up. "That was so cool. Most fun I've had in a long time. We should do that again," he said.

"Yeah, well I'm sure Hugh has a million ideas. We can make a new movie every week, or turn it into a series. You guys can come over anytime,"

Lilli reinforced her own status as possessing an apartment on Market Street, a coveted position that most of the kids aspired to, including her, before she had one of her own. All three were about Lilli's age. Jack was the only one of the three who lived with both parents. The other two lived with single moms, more the norm than not in Little Heart.

"See you, Peep," they said, itching to roll.

"Take care," Lilli had adopted this parting phrase, emulating what she had heard from some of the twenty-somethings. She thought it sounded more refined than the typical Market Street goodbye: 'Later.' The boys dropped their boards and shot across the street, stopping traffic with a screeching of brakes that made them laugh hysterically. They responded to angry honking by flipping the bird at the cars and continuing, laughing all the way up the street.

Lilli continued on to the deli and got two cups of coffee with milk. She liked hers with sugar, but Hugh drank it with just milk, so she had adapted. Learning to like the things that Hugh liked was a conscious goal of hers. In some ways, she felt like being with Hugh gave her access to the older Little Heart scene, to all of the tastes and lifestyles of those who had passed teenager-hood and had, in her mind, become elite simply by surviving into their twenties.

Walking back up the street, she saw Ella crossing over with her dog and groaned internally. She used to think Ella was harmless, but after she slept with the Sandler, leading to Lilli's spiral into misery, she gained an enormous distrust and dislike of her. Ella had good pot, though, so Lilli tried to keep things smooth with her.

"Hi, Lilli!" Ella acted as if they were good friends, but Lilli knew better.

"Hey, Ella," she replied with a lukewarm smile.

"How's your *old* man," Ella asked with a sideways smile.

"He's cool, sleeping still. We were up late making a movie, and then watching the tower burn. Oh, that's right. We saw you and Zep up on the field last night. Crazy, huh?"

Ella's smile faltered. "Yeah, pretty crazy."

"Zep still in town? I know Hugh wanted to hang out with him today before he leaves, if he's around."

"Yeah, he went to see Raiche at the Trash House. I think he's coming back in a little while. I'll tell him to come over."

"Just send us a smoke signal across the street!" Lilli joked. Ella's apartment was directly across Market Street. Lilli's bedroom window actually looked into Ella's living room.

"Okay, I'll send you a *smoke* signal," Ella put her thumb and pointer together, miming toking on a joint. Lilli laughed, thinking that she herself would be a lot more subtle if she were the biggest pot dealer in Little Heart. "Later, Lilli," Ella said, walking away with Kelpie at her heels. That dog never wore a leash but somehow never strayed from Ella's side.

"Take care," said Lilli.

Lilli put one cup of coffee down on the step

and pulled open the street door, which opened to the flight of stairs leading to her apartment. As she struggled to prop open the door with her back while reaching for the cup she had put down, she heard rustling at the top of the stairs and looked up, surprised to see Finn standing outside of her apartment door.

"Did you forget something?" Lilli called up as she climbed the stairs.

"Oh, there you are Lil," said Finn, looking uncomfortable.

"Where's Ro?"

"He's with Mom. I needed to talk to you."

"What's up?"

"I just came to say 'I'm sorry.' You were doing me a favor, and I treated you like crap. So...I'm sorry."

Lilli was suspicious. "It's okay, I mean, I kind of screwed up. I'm not really a good babysitter."

"I know," said her sister, "but I knew that when I left Kairo with you, and I should have given you better instructions."

This was a sister she didn't recognize. "Yeah, well, you were kind of too busy lecturing me," said Lilli.

"Yeah, I'm sorry about that, too. You're right. You're not me, and you may be fine doing exactly what you're doing. I just worry about you sometimes and want to spare you the shit I've gone through."

"I've been through my own shit, Finn. You have no idea." Finn had been so preoccupied with raising a baby and struggling with her addictions in the past few years that she had not seemed to even notice Lilli's life-or-death crisis. "It's better now, though. Actually, it's better now than it's ever been," said Lilli.

"I'm happy for you. Hugh's a nice guy. It makes me nervous that he's so much older, and I'm just afraid you're going to get hurt, but he does seem to really care about you."

"Yeah, he does, Finn. I'm glad you see that."

"Okay, well, I gotta get back home. Mom's going out, and I have to watch Josey." Finn hugged her awkwardly, but with Lilli's hands full with the two cups of coffee, she couldn't really hug back.

"Hey, could you open the door for me before you go," Lilli requested.

"Sure," said Finn, and reached for the door, holding it open for her sister. "See you later, Lil. Love you."

"Love you, too, Finnie. Take care."

Lilli went inside and back to the room she shared with Hugh. "Hughey, wake up," she said softly. Hugh cracked an eye and grumbled. "I brought you coffee," she said. Hugh sat up on one elbow and looked toward the window.

"Shit, what time is it?" he asked.

"Close to five. You slept all day, but then, we didn't get to bed until late. I don't even know what time you went to sleep. You were still editing the movie when I crashed. Did you finish it?"

"Mostly. I need to look at it again today and do a few more things, but it's almost done. I didn't go to sleep until almost eight in the morning," he said.

"Shit. No wonder you slept all day," she said.

"What happened to Kairo? Wasn't he here?"

"Yeah, Finn picked him back up. I forgot I was supposed to watch him today. He wanted to see you, but you were asleep." Lilli handed Hugh the coffee. He took off the lid and drank most of it in one big sip.

"Where's my camera? I want to finish one thing quickly on that tape." Hugh looked around and then fixated on the end of the bed. Lilli had forgotten the tapes, the spaghetti nightmare. "What the....?" Hugh opened his mouth and Lilli quickly started explaining.

"It was Kairo, but it wasn't his fault. I fell back to sleep. I'll fix them, I'll straighten it all out and wind them all back up," Lilli was not sure how Hugh would react. He was usually easygoing, but he was a little neurotic about his music and equipment.

"Damn it, some of those are originals with no copies. If the tape got damaged at all..."

"I don't think any of it got ripped, it's just all tangled up. I'll fix it," Lilli repeated, setting down her coffee and beginning to start detangling the mess. She stopped when she noticed that Hugh's video camera was lying off to the side of the pile. She had not seen it earlier. The deck was opened and with dread, Lilli saw the video tape nearby. It was the one that held the contents of the alien movie.

"Oh, no," Lilli said. She held up the tape, unwound into curls and floppy knots surrounding it, and showed it to Hugh. Hugh looked at it wordlessly, and Lilli watched Hugh's face, holding her breath.

"Lilli..." he said in a serious tone. Lilli sat frozen. "...let's not have any kids," he said, and cracked a huge smile. They both started laughing.

Chapter 4: The List

Finn Endicott

Finn drove down the long driveway to her mom's house. Toward the back of the property was the trailer where she lived. Her mom had put the trailer in when Finn had Kairo, to keep them nearby, but also so that they could have their own place, too. Her mom was like that, respecting her space, but also wanting her close.

She walked in the front door of her mom's house. Josey and Kairo were playing on the floor, surrounded by blocks and random cooking utensils. They were born less than five months apart, and had grown up together, seeing each other every day, so were more like siblings than anything else. Her mother, Evelyn, was in the kitchen, wiping counters and cleaning up after the kids' dinner.

"Hey, Finnie! Good, you're home. I gotta run. I

fed the kids, there's a bowl of minestrone left here for you, I'm taking the rest to the potluck."

"Okay," said Finn.

"I'll be back in a few hours if you want to put them to bed down here. Gotta go save the world, or at least…" she looked like she was trying to remember which part of the world needed saving today, "Nicaragua!" She kissed Finn and then the kids on the top of their heads quickly before running out the door with her big pot wrapped in a towel.

Josey and Kairo were still playing contentedly, so Finn went into the kitchen and picked up the phone. She dialed Janie, her sponsor.

"I did it," she told her when she picked up.

"How did it feel?" the husky voice on the other end asked. Janie had been Finn's sponsor since the first day she walked into a meeting six months ago.

"It was okay. She accepted my apology," Finn said.

"No, how did it *feel?*"

"Um… it felt…kind of embarrassing, but I felt good afterward. I was glad I went back. I think her feelings really had been hurt. She's really still just a kid, even though she's out on her own with that guy now. "

"That was Step Ten, Finnian, when you are wrong, promptly admitting it. It makes it easier not to carry baggage from one day to the next in sobriety. We have enough baggage from our past that we don't need to create more in recovery."

"Wow, I'm up to Step Ten already?"

"No, Finn, you're not up to Step Ten, you worked Step Ten today. I know we've talked about this before, but it's worth repeating because it's really important. The steps are a little deceiving because even though you can work them sequentially, and that makes sense, you're not really done when you get to Twelve. You work different steps depending on the situation and where you are in your recovery. You stop when you die, and if you stop earlier, well... you'll probably go back to drinking. Sorry, Hun, you don't get to graduate from this one."

"So then, what step are you working on?" Finn tested.

"Right now I'm working Step Twelve, carrying the message to another alcoholic... You," Janie replied promptly.

"Oh."

"What are you going to do tonight?" asked Janie.

"Put the kids to bed, my mom is at a potluck so I have Josey, too, go do some homework, then go to bed, I guess."

"Okay, I also want you to make a gratitude list," Janie said.

"A gratitude list?"

"Yes, what you're grateful for. What went right today, at least five things," explained Janie.

"Okay... you're pretty bossy, you know that?" said Finn, laughing for the first time that day.

"That's why you love me," said Janie.

Finn said goodnight and hung up. It *was* why she loved Janie. She was so paralyzed, so numb, so confused, that it was a relief for someone to just tell her what to do sometimes. She had picked Janie as a sponsor because she was the first to approach her after her first meeting. She came up and hugged her and asked her what meeting she was going to the next day. Finn didn't even know how she had gotten to that meeting, but the question helped her actually get to one the next day, too. Janie met her there and nudged her along, checking on her, holding her accountable, being motherly, stern, and playful, all at once. It was exactly what Finn needed. Janie was also one of the few sober Black women who went to the meetings in the area.

Finn often fantasized what it would have been like to be raised by Janie instead of by her White mother. Finn's father was Black, but she never knew him. Her mother had told her that he was an activist that she had met down south and fallen in love with during the Civil Rights Movement who had died while she was pregnant in '63. Evelyn had never made any connections to his family, though, and had always evaded all inquiries about him. Finn was named after him. His name had been Finnian Endicott, too, but that was all Evelyn would ever tell her. When Finn would ask why she couldn't reach out to his family, Evelyn tensed up and teared up. She would say that it would be hurtful to them, that they didn't know that Finn even existed. Once Evelyn let it slip that Finn's father didn't even know she was pregnant when he died.

Evelyn kept so much secrecy around it that

eventually Finn stopped asking for explanations. Her mother was generally a pretty open person, but this was something that she was just unwilling to talk about. Evelyn had embraced Finn's difference, had bought her books on African American culture, made sure she had children's books with Black characters, Black dolls, and even a few Black friends, although there was not much of a selection in Little Heart. She didn't realize that by doing this, Finn felt more different, not less.

Finn had always felt outside of everything. She somehow believed she should know innately about the Black world, but had no real connection to it. Still, the White world perceived her and treated her as separate and apart from it. She was caught in limbo, the White world seeing her as Black, the Black world, she felt, not accepting her as genuinely Black. She felt like she could never blend into one or the other world. When she did interact with Black people, she was stiff and uncomfortable, feeling like she did not know the rules. It had gotten better over the years, but she still felt like she did not belong anywhere.

Janie helped a little, with her big warm hugs, straight talk, and tough love. She was on the heavier side, and always dressed up in beautiful outfits, long dresses, color coordinated skirts and embroidered shirts with elaborate lace and beading. She wore her short grey hair in little dreads with a few beads here and there. She was the first person to actually play with Finn's hair. Evelyn had never really known what to do with it, and Finn had been kind of left on her own to figure it out. She had experimented with oils and relaxers and straighteners, sneaking home mysterious bottles and boxes from the pharmacy. She would try to decipher the instructions on her own, suffering the chemical burns and mistakes when she screwed it up. Then, as a teen she had started wearing it in dreadlocks, which had helped her when she lived on Market Street selling pot. It was kind of like advertisement, since White folk associated dreads with Rastafarianism and weed. People liked buying pot from the girl with the long blonde dreads. It made it seem more authentic to them, as if she had gone herself to Jamaica to grow, harvest, and smuggle the weed back herself.

Finn got to witness the exposed ugly underside of people's ignorance and racism, which they were never even smart enough or tactful enough to disguise. It made her want to divorce herself from all things White, from the poverty of understanding she experienced as the air around her. Despite her disdain, she had her own roots in White culture. After all, here she was, half-White, raised by a White woman, a single mother living in a trailer. Janie confronted her on this, made her talk about it and express her discomfort. For the first time, she was talking about her feelings about being an outsider with someone, and realizing how hurt she had been by it. Janie was patient and didn't judge Finn for the things she thought she should know but didn't, or the strange ideas she had.

"How would you know?" Janie asked her.

"I feel like I'm supposed to just know," Finn admitted.

"That's bullshit. Look, it's like being a mother. We think we're supposed to just know what to do with these little buggers, but they don't come with instructions. We do the best we can, and then spend the rest of our lives trying to make up for it. It's like with my son. I never really raised him. I was drunk and smoking crack and chasing this man or that man, leaving him with whoever would take him. I was limited by my addiction and my own childhood experience. My mother wasn't there for me, either, so how could I know how to be there for my son? It was the best I had to offer him at the time, even though it wasn't good enough. Now I have to make up for it by being present, accepting responsibility for how that affected him. Your mother did the best she could, but she didn't know any better either. How would she?"

It made sense, and helped Finn forgive her mother for not knowing how to teach her how to be Black, or even how to be successfully biracial. Her mother was naïve and didn't know what she was doing, but she really did try her best. But then, how could she deny Finn relationships with her father's family? That could have helped, having a grandma and maybe aunts and uncles and cousins that looked more like her. Finn realized that Evelyn probably had her own reasons for avoiding those relationships, but she still held on to the resentment about this loss of family connection. Janie said they would work on this in the later steps.

In the meantime, Finn just put one foot in front

of the other, and tried not to dwell on it, but everything seemed amplified X 100. She was still just having trouble clearing her head. Janie called it *mocus,* short for "mostly out of focus." Her brain did feel foggy, but then her emotions were all over the place, too. She was irritable and impatient with Kairo, and tended to be snappy with others, hence what had happened with Lilli that afternoon. She was just really... uncomfortable. She heard other people talking about their experiences in early recovery, and knew that this was something that was common and would get better with some time. She listened to that, and clung to the idea that what she was going through was temporary, and that every day it would get a little easier. She held on to the hope that one day she would intuitively know how to handle the things that baffled her now. She hadn't seen that happen yet, but she knew she hated herself a little less than when she had been drinking every day.

"Come on kids, time to clean up. We're going up to our house." Finn coached Josey and Kairo to clean up the toys and then started searching for shoes and coats. "Where are your shoes, Josey?" She located them and then began fighting with Josey's feet, trying to shove the shoes on without untying the laces. She cursed under her breath and mumbled, forcing the shoes on roughly. Josey yelped a little and pulled her foot back. "I'm sorry, Josey, I didn't mean to hurt you," she said.

She looked up and saw Josey's sweet little forgiving smile. "It's okay, Finnie" she said. Finn untied the shoes and started over, more gently this time.

She lugged Kairo on her hip and held Josey's hand walking up the sidewalk to the trailer in the fading light. She snapped on some lights and told the kids to go play in Kairo's room. "I'll be in to read to you in a little bit, so make sure you pick out some books." The kids were so used to being together in one house or the other, sharing toys, beds, mothers. They squabbled sometimes, but mostly they got along and enjoyed each other's company. They were rarely separated. Finn was already pregnant when her mother had gone back to work after maternity leave, so she had stayed home with Josey. When she had Kairo, shortly after, she and her mother worked out an arrangement; Finn had the babies all day and then her mother took over when she got home from work. Finn's mom didn't have to pay for childcare for Josey, and Finn got to go out at night.

That was when she had started drinking again. She had stopped while she was pregnant, but after Kairo's dad left, she felt so lonely and distressed that she wanted to be with people when her mom got home to relieve her. She didn't have her own car, so she would borrow her mom's. Evelyn went to bed early with the kids, and never really knew what time Finn got home. She would drop the kids off in the morning, and Finn would get up and guzzle some coffee and try to function until nap time when she could catch up on sleep she hadn't gotten the night before. Juggling two little babies all day was exhausting by itself, but with a hangover, it was downright deadly. She somehow still found energy to go out in the evening and do it all over again. Some nights she was too beat up to go anywhere, but would leave the kids down at her mom's anyway, get high and watch movies by herself.

Evelyn knew that Finn smoked and drank some, but since she was always able to take care of the kids in the morning, she decided to leave Finn alone about it. She was, after all, an adult. Evelyn also needed Finn. Having already raised two daughters entirely by herself, she was relieved to have help with Josey. Josey's father was an old flame that had lived with Evelyn on and off when Lilli was still pretty young and Finn was a teenager already. He was a drunk, unreliable, but charming in his own way, and when he showed back up for a few months every once in a while, Evelyn would get pulled back in until he took off again.

This last time, after finding out she was pregnant, he disappeared in the middle of the night with Evelyn's entire paycheck. Evelyn tracked him down shortly afterward. He was selling socks at flea markets down south with some drinking cronies. That was apparently more appealing than a 40-year old knocked-up girlfriend he had no intention of marrying. A few months after Josey was born, police showed up at 4:00 A.M. and informed her that he had been killed down in Florida. An old license with Evelyn's address was the only identification he had in his wallet. Ironically, he had been walking home from buying beer at the convenience store and had been hit by a drunk driver.

Evelyn, not having a dad around for Josey, and

Finn, not having a dad around for Kairo, had brought the two closer in some ways. Like many co-parents, though, it kept the focus on the kids, their needs, and shifting responsibilities, and they often missed each other in the transitions from one house to the next. Evelyn missed Finn's deterioration, her desperation, and even the most basic aspects of Finn's personal life. It was kind of like how she totally missed Finn's struggle with her biracial identity. Evelyn was preoccupied by her work, running a literacy program for children of migrant farm workers, and by her various political endeavors and intermittent romantic dramas.

When it was her turn to watch the kids, she went to bed with them early and didn't notice the cars that left in the morning or when Finn didn't come home until the next day. She did not even notice when Finn's "friend" Shara started sleeping over lots of nights, and did not think anything of it when Kairo started calling her "Mommy Snake." This was a short-lived relationship, since Shara got fed up with Finn's drinking and flirting with men in front of her, and eventually she ended it. This had actually been part of the impetus for Finn getting sober. She had sunk to new lows in the few months following Shara's leaving her.

Finn had burned every remaining bridge of friendship in the town in her final night of drinking by bringing home not one, but two people who she should not have been sleeping with. One was the boyfriend of a friend, who just happened to be around drinking that night, and the other was the current girlfriend of Kairo's father. Her name was

Dylan. Dylan had been with Kairo's dad, Jake, for two years, and Finn had been infatuated with her for that whole time. She had quickly gotten over her hurt feelings over Jake leaving her and Kairo when he returned from the West Coast with Dylan. She was the most unusual creature Finn had ever seen. She had a spindly, boyish figure, high cheekbones, a green mohawk that she wore flopped down to one side, and clothes patched up with leather stitched together with dental floss. She held her head high and stared directly into Finn's eyes, unapologetic for being her replacement. When Finn met Dylan, she told Jake, "Watch out, I'm going to steal her from you."

Jake characteristically flashed his sheepish grin and said, "Please do." He had always teased Finn that she was a dyke, and had encouraged her to experiment with women while they were together.

A circuitous courtship and romance with Dylan followed, but she was never able to fully disentangle her from Jake's magnetic hold. Finn held on to the fantasy that she would whisk Dylan away and marry her. Her relationship with Dylan over the next few years was laced with poignant yearning, drunken binges, and many close encounters, but although they had kissed a few times, they had never ended up sleeping together. That night, though, somehow ended with this random tagalong boyfriend and much tequila under their belts. Rather than being a titillating ménage a trois, it was one of the most humiliating nights of Finn's life.

Dylan was surprisingly aggressive, almost hostile

with Finn, and the random boy kept poking himself in. Dylan would not let him touch her, so he focused on Finn, too, attacking her from the other side. Finn was too drunk to even figure out that he did not belong there. Nothing could have been less sexy. She had always thought that being with Dylan would be different, like two halves of a soul coming together, not the angry mixed-up jumble it became. After waking up from that ugly night, with Dylan impatiently dismissing her to return to Jake, the random boy dismissing her to go confess to his upset girlfriend, and half the town mad at her, Finn admitted defeat and started going to meetings. Having her long-standing fantasy about Dylan shattered, her motivation now was to win Shara back and prove to her that she could stay clean and be a good loyal girlfriend.

Finn was back in school. She had gotten kicked out of high school for selling pot eight years earlier and had never returned. After she first got sober, she had quickly taken the test for her equivalency diploma and was now enrolled in the local community college. She did some homework, read to the kids and put them to bed. She stared at a blank page in her journal, wrote 'Gratitude' on the top, listed the numbers one through five on separate lines, and then called Janie.

"What is it now?" Janie's sleepy voice said.

"I don't know what to write. I'm not grateful for anything."

"You can't think of even one thing?"

"No," replied Finn.

"How're the kids?" Janie asked.

"They're in bed... they're sleeping."

"Are you grateful for that?"

"Yeah, I guess so."

"Are your lights on?"

"Yes."

"Are you grateful for that?"

"Really? I'm supposed to write things like that? That my lights are on? That seems kind of silly."

"Well, you don't have any ideas, so you may need to start small, your lights, food in your fridge, your house being warm, kids safe in bed, you get the picture."

"Okay, if you think so," Finn was skeptical.

"Good. Work on that and call me in the morning. G'night, Finn," Janie did not wait for Finn to respond before hanging up.

Finn looked at the page for a few more minutes and then wrote:

1. Kids safe
2. Janie
3. Being in school
4. Being sober, no hangover tomorrow!
5. Second chances

Part II:

November 10 – 12, 1988

Chapter 5: Honey

Sadie

Sadie watched her boots as she walked up Chapel Street. Her army green fatigues swaddled her thick legs with multiple pockets and zippers. She had worked late at the deli. It was dark already and the street lights were on, washing the sidewalks with a phosphorescent stillness that reminded Sadie of the miniature towns that populated model train sets. She was headed to Ella's with her cashed paycheck in her pocket. It had been a long week, plagued with thoughts of the last weekend's bender and trying to sort out the missing puzzle pieces to her strange night out.

Eddie, an old hippie that worked in the tie dye factory, came into the deli on Monday to check on her.

"How you doin' today, Sweetness?" he asked.

"Great, Eddie, how about you?"

"I was really worried about you on Friday."

"You were?"

"Well, yeah, you were so wasted, I didn't think you could make it home."

"You saw me on Friday?"

"Don't you remember? That's how you ended up in my apartment. I was down on the street with Jack and Ditto and we were headed back to my place to smoke a bowl and you came stumbling out of the Pub, around closing time. We could tell there was no way you could make it home, so the three of us helped you upstairs. You didn't even smoke with us, you just passed right out."

"Shit, Eddie. I don't even remember. I just remember waking up there, but I didn't know it was your place. Well, that makes me feel better. Thank you."

He gave her a big hairy kiss. "No problem, Sugar. Someone needs to look out for the fair maidens of Market Street. There are a lot of creeps in this town who would take advantage of a drunk girl." He raised his furry eyebrows and gave Sadie a knowing look, letting her know he was referring to Raiche.

Sadie reflected on that as she walked, wondering why the world seemed to be made up only of nice old smelly guys and sparkly young dangerous ones. The old smellies just wanted a little love, but all they could ever really hope for was to occasionally divert danger away from the young lasses who stumbled around, drunk, blinded, and dazzled by the sparklies.

Her calves ached going up the hill to the back of Ella's apartment, but she remembered her last trip up that hill, and was grateful to be in a clearer state of mind. She could hear loud music from inside the apartment. The door was propped and she pushed it the rest of the way open to be blasted with warm, smoky air, beer vapor, and bone-grinding thrash. Too late, she recognized Raiche's squealing guitar and reverberating feedback. She forgot. She had heard that Preying Menace was playing that night at Ella's. She wanted to avoid seeing Raiche, but feeling pressure to honor her promise to pay Ella Friday and return her clothes, and also hoping to score an additional bag, she went on in. Her heart pounded in competition with the resounding bass.

Jack and Ditto were standing in the hallway, collecting money for the keg. "Hey look, it's Sadie *Lain!* Hi Sadie *Lain!*" they shouted in chorus.

"Yeah, yeah, you two are fucking hysterical!" Sadie yelled over the music.

"Three bucks," said Jack and held his hand out.

"I'm just here to see Ella for a minute, idiots. I'm not paying for the keg," she was annoyed by these sniveling youngsters, even if they had helped to rescue her from the streets the week before.

"It's three bucks, Sadie *Lain,*" they repeated.

Sadie ignored them and shouldered past them into the crowded kitchen. She looked back to see them with wide, comical faces of open-mouthed surprise, shouting curses, and wildly gesticulating behind her, but pushed on. She saw Ella across the sea of leather jackets and bobbing heads, with an old bass player from one of the previous decade's local bands hanging on her and speaking closely into her ear. Ella smiled and leaned toward him, with a plastic cup in one hand. Ella's other hand, Sadie observed, was extended and holding on to the hand of the boy with the mohawk, Darien, who Sadie had seen there the week before. Darien was slumped down, sitting sulkily on the floor with his back against the wall. He looked like a little kid holding on to his mother's skirt. Ella extricated her hand, and Darien groped after her, but she moved away with the old guitar player, escaping into her bedroom.

Sadie could see Raiche, flailing on his knees prostrating his guitar in front of the other members of the Menace. She was glad he was preoccupied and would not notice her. To one side, on the couch that Sadie had dozed on the week before, sat Lilli and Hugh, watching the antics. Lilli looked like an angry little doll, propped up next to Hugh in a short green dress splattered with big funky flowers and green tights with little pointy shoes. Sadie envied Lilli for her tiny little frame and porcelain features. She knew about the sordid history between Lilli and Raiche, having heard Raiche's side of the episode at the Trash House, how Lilli had begged to be handcuffed and fucked by whoever would "do" her. Now, knowing Raiche a little better, she wondered about this version of the story. She knew Lilli was promiscuous, but couldn't picture this contained little person begging to be tied up. She wondered how Lilli felt, sitting there with her boyfriend, one of Raiche's best friends, while Raiche strutted his monstrous ego before them.

Seeing Hugh was not comfortable for Sadie, either. She had a fling with him earlier that summer. They had hooked up in the back of his drummer's car one hot July evening after drinking wine coolers all day. It was embarrassing for both of them, she guessed, since he had overtly avoided her since then. He always nodded cordially and said hello, but ducked his head away quickly whenever he encountered her. Tonight he was grinning ear to ear, watching his friend and thrashing his head to the music, oblivious to anything except the guitar god before him. Hugh had his own band with Raiche, but seemed to be ecstatic just to see his friend play with this competing band. He did not even seem to be aware of Lilli, who he jostled and bumped with his enthusiastic movements. She sat stiffly next to him, with glaring eyes on Raiche. Next to Hugh, with his big frame and boisterous energy, Lilli looked even smaller and younger.

Sadie edged through the crowd and made her way to Ella's bedroom door, which was closed. She was about to knock but then, remembering that the old bass player was in there with her, thought better of it. At that moment, the door opened, though, and the guy walked out, tucking a bag of weed into his shirt pocket. Ella was following behind him, but when she saw Sadie, her face lit up and she ushered Sadie in and closed the door. The sound dissolved behind the closed door, muffled, but still frighteningly loud in Ella's room. Sadie had never been in there before and looked around at the tapestries, strings of Christmas lights, and at the closet where the futon-bed was tucked away, Ella's infamous Lair. Ella's dog, Kelpie, was lying back in the lair with her head on her paws, trying to get as far away from the noise as possible.

"Hey, Ella. Yeah, so I just wanted to bring you your clothes and pay you for that bag last week, and maybe get another eighth," Sadie started handing her the bag of clothes. Ella nodded, but seemed distracted and motioned for Sadie to sit down on a U-shaped loveseat. It was olive green satin and looked like it should be in the boudoir of a courtesan. Sadie put the bag of clothes on a small table and sat down. She felt pronounced discomfort sitting on such an elaborate piece of furniture, feeling rough and out of place in her boots and army drab. She had a flash fantasy where she was a big coarse soldier coming out of the field to visit some delicate flower of a prostitute in a remote country. She brushed off this confusing daydream and noticed that Ella was standing in her closet-bed, lit up by the ruby glow of the strings of lights, and reaching up into the folds of tapestries. For a moment, she saw what all the boys seemed to see in Ella; someone seductive, mysterious, and unattainable, no matter how physically available she made herself. Sadie pushed these thoughts away.

Ella came out and tossed a bag of weed to Sadie. "Here you go, new batch from Aurora this week. Very kind. Even better than the last batch."

"Oh, thanks," Sadie said and fumbled with some bills and handed them to Ella, who tossed them into a little urn without counting them. "Listen, do you mind if I smoke in here before I go back out there?"

"Of course not, as long as you share!" Ella laughed. Sadie pulled some papers out of her jacket pocket and took the tray Ella handed to her. It was a long rectangle made out of swirled purple, gray, and green glass that looked like it was made just for rolling.

"I forgot Menace was playing tonight. I wasn't really happy to see Raiche, you know?" admitted Sadie.

There was a knock at the door and Darien stood in the doorway. Ella rushed over and said a few things Sadie couldn't hear over the blast of music that followed him in, then pushed him back out the door and closed it.

"He's really starting to get on my nerves. I've got to ditch him," she said, shaking her head. "He's clingy. And... he bites. I know he thinks it's sexy, but he's starting to really hurt me, and it's just annoying." She plopped down on the floor on a big cushion next to Sadie's chair and then looked over at the sticky green buds Sadie was extricating from the stems and seeds. "Can I have the seeds? I send them back to Aurora," she explained.

"Uh, sure," said Sadie, and Ella scooped up the dozen or so seeds and put them in a little bowl on a shelf.

"He's got this pull with people," Ella said. "He sucks women in and then gets high off of hurting them." It took Sadie a minute to realize she was talking about Raiche. She had started to think Ella had not heard what she had said, or had gotten distracted by Darien coming in. "I've watched him do it for years. But it's not just the women. He does it with men, too. Look at Hugh, totally smitten with him. You'd think he was in love with him. I mean, he is pretty sexy, so I understand the attraction, but he's got bad news written all over him. You'd have to be a masochist to play with that ball of string."

"Yeah, I found that out the hard way, but then maybe I'm a masochist," Sadie said.

"No, I don't think you're a masochist, I think you just fell for the oldest trick in the book," said Ella.

"What's that?" Sadie asked.

"You know, getting pulled in to someone's web just because they're flashy and charismatic. Have you ever read Jane Austen?"

"Um, no. Wasn't she some frumpy old Victorian romance writer or something?"

"Jane Austen is the opposite of a romance writer, Sadie! In all her books there are these dashing young fellows that come in and sweep the ladies off their feet. Every one of those suckers gets her heart broken. The steadfast boring guys, the ones that are bookworms, or grumpy, or have bad social skills, they turn out to be the real heroes, and the girls who hold out for the boring steady guys, they're the ones who end up happy. The ones who get snaked and fall for the dazzlers, they end up broken and miserable."

Sadie thought back about her reflections on

Eddie and how she had just been thinking something very similar. "So then, I should go after the boring steady guys?"

"Yeah, or maybe the boring steady girls," Ella said and winked.

Sadie flushed. "I told you, I'm not into that! Last week was a fluke. I was really wasted. Shit, Ella, now I'm sorry I even told you!"

"Hey, don't get mad, Sadie... Get high!" Ella laughed and took the joint Sadie had rolled off the tray. She produced the same little blue foil lighter from the week before and lit up, inhaling deeply and passing the joint to Sadie. "No really, I was just kidding, Sadie. I know you like boys... like Raiche. You'll be just fine."

Sadie couldn't tell if Ella was making fun of her, so she decided to just leave it alone. She had these glimmers where she felt like Ella really liked her and then times she seemed to be just playing with her. Maybe like Darien, Ella just didn't know when she bit too hard.

There was a lull in the music and Raiche came bursting in, looking for Ella. He pushed up intimately to her and whispered in her ear. Ella laughed and said something back to him that Sadie couldn't hear. He turned to go back out and finally seemed to notice Sadie. "Hey, Sadie," he said, turning his mocking smile toward her. Sadie's heart flipped and she stumbled, not wanting to give him the satisfaction of even acknowledging him, but unable to help herself.

"Hi," she managed to get out.

"What are you doing later?" Sadie could not

believe how bold this little bastard was.

"Uh, just hanging out, nothing really," she said.

"You should stop by later. I want to show you something."

"Oh, okay, I guess so," she could not believe this was happening and that she was responding in this way.

"I've been wanting to talk to you. Come by my house later, okay?"

"Yeah, okay, I'll see you later," Sadie replied.

Raiche turned and bolted out, and a few moments later the music started up again.

"Hissssss!!!" Ella said to Sadie, miming a snake about to strike.

"Oh, shut up, Ella," Sadie said.

♦ ♦ ♦

Several hours later, Sadie trudged back up the hill toward Ella's house. The party was over. It was well after midnight, but Ella's lights were still on, and she could see her moving around inside from the window facing Market Street. She went up the back alley and Kelpie, who was sitting on the back stoop, barked a welcoming hello as Sadie approached.

Ella opened the door. "C'mon Kelp," she called. Then she noticed Sadie. "Oh, hey Sadie! What are you doing out here in the dark?"

"I just got here. I saw your lights were on."

"Well, come in. I'm up. Everyone's gone, I was just cleaning up."

"I'll help," said Sadie.

They finished picking up the plastic cups discarded all over the apartment, dumping the dredges in the sink and picking up cigarette butts and crushed empty packs, throwing them in a big black trash bag. Sadie was reminded of her wedding dress.

"I don't know why I agree to these things," Ella said. "I'll finish cleaning up tomorrow. C'mon, let's do a bong hit."

"Okay," said Sadie, feeling a little crispy around the edges, but thinking that might be just the thing to mellow her out.

They sat on Ella's living room couch and Ella produced a little plastic honey bear that had been turned into a bong and started stuffing its bowl with green bud.

Sadie laughed. "That's cute," she said, gesturing to the bear.

"Oh, you like Fred? Yeah, he's a good friend, I even wrote a song about him." Ella started to sing: *"My honey bear bong, Oh, my honey bear bong. I love you so much, I wrote this song!"* She started cracking up, finished packing the bowl, and toked up, handing it to Sadie.

"That's funny," said Sadie, taking Fred and following suit.

"Hey, I finally got rid of Darien. He, of course, stuck around after everyone left, grabbing at me. I had to tell him it's over. I couldn't handle another night. I can't afford a Tetanus shot."

"How did he take it?"

"He's such a baby. I mean, he knows I see other people, but he acted like I promised him something. I said, 'Look, honey, you need to expand your horizons. I'm holding you back from discovering some great girl who's going to make you happy.' He stormed around and cried a little bit, but then he left, thank god."

"Yeah, well, he *is* kind of a baby. He's what, fifteen?"

"Point well taken, Sadie. A mistake I will never make again. You'd think two years age difference would not be so vast, but he's still sucking on his mommy's tit. I just became the new mommy! Men are pretty two-dimensional, Sadie. I didn't really grow up with them, so they're interesting to me, but the more research I do, the more I realize there's not really much there. They're fun to play with, but very few get past their own cocks into any level of deeper thinking."

Sadie was a little surprised. She had always assumed Ella really liked men, since she hung out with them so much.

"So, it's just a game to you?" Sadie asked.

"Well, I'm amused by them, let's put it that way. There are a few I like to fuck, a few I really admire, like Zep, and then a few I am fascinated with, like Raiche. It's like watching a spider catch something in his web and then suck all the blood out of it. He's a true predator. It's pretty interesting, like watching a nature show. By the way, little fly, how did you do tonight?"

"Well, I don't think I got my blood sucked out, or maybe I did, I don't know," Sadie was still trying to process what happened.

"Do you *feel* like you got your blood sucked out?"

"I don't know, maybe. Are you going to tease me? I don't know if I can handle that right now," she said, unsure she could cope with Ella's taunting. Sadie suspected that Ella just liked watching her squirm.

"Well, I do find it very interesting that you know exactly what you're getting with Raiche, but still go back for more. Aren't you at all curious about why you might do that?"

"No, I know why I did it. I mean, I didn't want to even see him or talk to him tonight, but then when he asked me to come over, I thought..."

"You thought he might be in love with you?"

"No, of course not. I just thought maybe he was interested in me after all and I might have overreacted to the posters."

"Hmmmm," said Ella, fixing Sadie with a long look.

"I mean, maybe I did... overreact," she looked to Ella for confirmation, but got nothing. "Maybe he was just proud of "doing" me and wanted to brag about it. Maybe it was his way of publicizing that we had been together, like spray painting a love message?"

"Is that what he told you?"

"Sort of. He told me he was just having fun and wanted everyone to see what a beautiful ass I have. He said it was a compliment."

"And the love message?"

"I don't know, I guess I just made that part up. Remember a few years ago when he was dating that girl, Kristi, and he spray painted 'I love you, Kristi' on the water tower? I thought that was so romantic at the time. I guess I started thinking maybe it was like that, just his way of letting everyone know we were together. Maybe that was silly."

"And are you together, now?"

"I don't know. I really don't. I mean, it was weeks ago when we first hooked up and the posters came out. He hasn't even tried to call me or talk to me since then. I assumed it was some awful plot to torment me, but then tonight..."

"You thought maybe you had it all wrong and the posters were a love message after all, like marking his territory? Instead of pissing on telephone poles, he pasted your ass on them." It did sound silly when Ella said it. Sadie could not respond. "So then, did you hook up with him again tonight?"

"Actually... no," said Sadie. "I was surprised, I thought he had asked me over there to try to fuck me again, but when I got there, he started showing me these drawings he'd done of me, from the photograph and from what he remembered. He started talking about how I have a beautiful body, and how voluptuous female forms are underappreciated these days."

Ella was nodding, knowingly.

"Then he asked if he could draw me... nude."

"So, you agreed," Ella filled in.

"Yes," she admitted. "I don't know why. I'm so self-conscious."

"Maybe it was just nice to have someone tell you how beautiful you are, especially if you're insecure about your body," Ella proposed.

"Yeah, it was."

"I don't know that you necessarily should have been so flattered that you stripped down to model for him, but it makes sense to me that you would feel grateful that someone found you attractive."

"Yeah, but then why didn't he want to sleep with me? After he was done, he thanked me and told me he needed to get up early."

"So, you were actually disappointed, then."

"Well, no, I didn't really want to sleep with him, but I feel more vulnerable having him draw me than if I had just fucked him," she realized this was true as she was saying it.

"Exactly."

"Huh?"

"You gave him more of yourself than when you slept with him. First he got you to sleep with him, then he got you to pose for him against your will, then after violating and publically embarrassing you, he got you to actually agree to pose for him."

"Oh." The reality of what Ella was implying was dawning on Sadie.

"Fascinating."

"Yeah, well, this all may be incredibly interesting to you, Ella, but it's my life and my feelings. I'm not just some creature for you to look at under a magnifying glass. You know, you're pretty insensitive. I don't know why I even talk to you," Sadie felt her ire rising and knew she was lashing out.

"Hey, Sadie... Listen, it's not really like that at all," said Ella. "I mean, I may be morbidly interested in your romantic demise, but I watch myself and everyone else with the same scrutiny. I grew up on an island surrounded by lesbians and Jane Austen novels. Men are kind of a novelty to me. Their antics and behavior, and how women respond, it's really bizarre to me." Ella's background was a well-known piece of gossip in Little Heart, but Sadie had never heard her talk about it before. "You know, I'm not immune to it either. Like this thing with Darien, what an idiot I was! I screw up all the time! I get myself into all kinds of binds, I just don't take it so seriously. Maybe looking at it all like a social experiment makes it easier to tolerate."

Sadie took this admission as an Ella-type apology. Ella continued: "I've been known to make an ass of myself, too, you know. I just try to keep it low-key and laugh it off when I can't. I know what people say about me, I just don't let it get under my skin that much. You can't spend your life worrying about what other people think about you," she said, shaking her head and taking another bong hit. The honey bear bubbled and oozed smoke. He was colored a yellowish brown inside, apparently from frequent use.

Ella passed Sadie the bong. She took a hit and held it, then exhaled. "I just wish I hadn't been so stupid. I walked right into it."

"Yeah, well, he's a slippery one. Why do you think I've never messed around with him? I like to be the one breaking hearts, I generally stay away from the ones who are heartless," she said.

"You really think Raiche is heartless?"

"Well, maybe not heartless, but cruel," said Ella.

"Raiche is kind of a guy's guy- he is more concerned with being able to show off for his friends what a fierce conqueror he is than worrying about who he hurts. Personally, I think all the men in this town really just want to fuck each other, but they're too repressed. It comes out in being misogynistic- hurting women is kind of a game to them and it's their way of psychically getting each other off. Raiche and all his friends play at it. They all want to be fearless enough to pull off the shit Raiche does, but most of them are too inhibited. So they edge him on and encourage him, and then he acts it out for them. They get to vicariously experience the high men get from hurting women without actually being the perpetrator. In a way, he's as much a victim as you are, Sadie," she said.

"I don't know if I buy any of that, and I don't think I'm a victim, either. I mean, I went over there willingly. I agreed to model for him."

"Yeah, but you didn't really want to. You felt like you should. He persuaded you. He's really good at persuading people to do things they don't want to do." This sounded almost sympathetic to Sadie.

"I'm a big girl, though. He didn't make me do anything."

Ella raised her eyebrows. "I think you underestimate how much power he has over you," she said. "If he came back right now and told you he wanted you to be his girlfriend, would you do it?"

Sadie reflected on this. "Yes, I guess I would. I really liked him." It was hard for her to acknowledge this.

"Well, what do you like about him?"

"I don't know. He's really hot in this dark sinister type of way, he's a great guitar player, he's creative. He has this really quirky sideways kind of smile, like he's laughing at you, but it feels okay, like you want to be important enough for him to notice you, even if it means he laughs at you. I don't know. I'm just drawn to him, I guess." She was really high and free-associating. Ella's strong weed and candid pushiness always seemed to get her to talk.

"Yeah, he is pretty hot," Ella agreed. "Too bad he's such a creep. He'd be fun to play with if I didn't think my ass would get stuck up on posters all over town!" Ella giggled and Sadie laughed, too. It felt good to laugh at herself. "You know, Sadie," said Ella, "you're really okay." Sadie was getting drowsy. The long night and all the weed was getting to her and she was yawning nonstop now. "You're sleepy- you want to crash here?" asked Ella.

"Um, do you mind?" Sadie was always surprised when Ella flip-flopped from brash to nurturing.

"No problem- I'll get you some blankets. And, I can tell you another bed-time story. I never finished telling you what happened with the Farm Boy from Iowa."

"Oh, yeah...Adam, right?"

"Yeah, Adam," said Ella. She ran to her room and came back with a pillow and a few blankets. Sadie stretched out and Ella sat on the edge of the couch by her feet. "Adam, Adam, Adam," said Ella, as if trying to figure out where to pick back up.

"I remember he came and proposed to you, you told him you weren't pregnant anymore, and he stuck around for a while. How long did he stay in town before heading back to Iowa?"

"It was only about a week," said Ella. "It all fell apart after a week, plus, he needed to get back to the farm, to help his grandfather."

"That's right, his grandfather raised him, right?"

"Yeah, his mom died when he was little, and I guess his dad eventually got remarried and moved out of state. He stayed with Grandpa Joe."

"And you really liked him, right? He wasn't just a science experiment to you?"

Ella laughed. "No, he wasn't just an experiment. I mean, maybe at first. We had some beautiful nights along the river in Iowa, he knew a lot about the stars, about nature. He was so down-to-earth in this really humble, no-nonsense type of way. I really liked him then, but of course, he was just another guy that I sent a letter to when I got home. I had a nice time with him, but didn't honestly think much of it. He was just a part of my plan. Then when he showed up in Little Heart, it was really unsettling. I mean, I think you know this about me, Sadie, but I'm kind of an open book. I don't make any apologies for the choices I make, and I live the way I want to live. The only reason I felt okay lying to him on paper was because he was anonymous to me. It was a strategy with no casualties that I could see." Ella sighed.

"You're kind of a lot like Raiche, Ella," said Sadie. Ella started. She looked like Sadie had stung her. "I mean, you use men the way Raiche uses women," Sadie said.

"I guess you could say that," said Ella, pondering. "Yeah, I guess that's true," she concurred.

"Sorry, I didn't mean to interrupt your story," said Sadie, uncomfortable that she might have offended Ella, even though that consideration was not generally mutually extended to her.

"No, you're right," said Ella. "I never thought about it like that, but I do kind of de-personalize my relationships with men. They are objects to me, and I guess that isn't so different from the way most men treat women, not just Raiche," she seemed to really be giving this some thought.

"Go on, so what happened with Adam?"

"Well, Adam was different. I really started to care about him. He was not at all like the other specimens I had encountered. See, there I go, objectifying again, Sadie, you sly little devil! You're right! He was a pretty unique *specimen*. I mean, I got to know him as a person instead of as a man, was what I guess was so different. I don't know how to explain this, but usually when I interact with men, even if I'm not sleeping with them, I am very aware that they view me as a potential sex object. I can sense this, I feel it so tangibly, that they might as well just broadcast their thoughts out loud. It defines our whole interaction and nothing real can ever transpire between us because our whole discourse is infused with their fantasies about me. When I laugh over a weed sale with a customer, he is thinking about licking my breasts, when I smoke a joint with him, in his mind he has his cock in my mouth. It's something I have just gotten used to, so I almost don't even notice it. I always took it for granted that there is nothing real that can ever happen between a man and a woman."

"Really, you think so?" Sadie sounded dubious.

"Mostly, with some rare exceptions," said Ella.

"Okay, so Adam was an exception."

"Yes. It took me totally off guard. I couldn't even figure it out at first. See, the fantasies that men usually have about me are so present in our conversation, that it actually protects me. It creates a natural barrier between us. He will never really be interested in who I am as a person, and that somehow keeps me safe. I know that the person I am deep down inside is totally out of reach, so no one can touch me and no one can hurt me. They do not really know *me,* so I am inaccessible to them, even if I fuck them. With Adam, all of a sudden I realized that he cut through all of that and was asking me questions, not questions he thought he should ask to get me to put out or make me feel safe with him, but questions about myself that he wanted to know because he was genuinely curious about me, about who I was and where I came from. It was so disorienting, Sadie. I suddenly felt so naked! Huh, isn't that funny? I felt naked with him because he did not see me as a sexual object!"

"Strange, yeah, I see what you mean," said Sadie.

"So, I got really shy! Not like me at all, I didn't know what to say to him, and I stumbled over my words. He would look directly at me, not at my body or at my face, but right into my eyes, as if he wanted to look right into my brain!" Ella shook her head. "Boy, it freaked me out!"

"So how did you handle it?"

"I kind of fell apart. I was like a little girl, I had no defenses! The only defense I had ever learned was how to manipulate men who wanted to sleep with me. Here was a man who really seemed to not be all that interested in sex, I mean, he'd hold my hand or kiss me, but it wasn't foreplay to him, it was genuine affection. I didn't know how to handle it."

"But you must have had that before, Ella, with all the men you've been with- no offense- but hasn't anyone ever loved you before?"

"Men have been infatuated with me, they've become attached to me, but I don't think any of them ever had any idea who I really am. It was always more about their fantasy about who they wanted me to be than about the real me."

"Wow, that's actually pretty sad," said Sadie.

"Really? What, that men project their fantasies of women onto them and don't really see who they are? It's not just me, Sadie. That's pretty much the state of all inter-sex relationships. You think you've ever had anyone love *you*, the real you and not just who they thought you were?"

"Well, no, but I don't know. That's different. I don't think I'm very… loveable," said Sadie.

"Now that's sad! Holy shit, Sadie! You think it's you? These fuckers fuck you over and chew you up and spit you out, and you actually think it's *you*!" Sadie started to see another side of Ella.

Maybe she wasn't cold after all, maybe she was just mad.

"Well, I mean, I know men have used me, but I guess... I just always think I deserve it. I go after it. Like with Raiche. I put myself in bad situations, so it's not really any surprise when men don't respect me."

"Oh, Sadie. You really need to go live on an island for a while! There's nothing wrong with you except that you have somehow let these pigs define you," said Ella.

"Isn't that what you do, let them 'project their fantasies' onto you? Doesn't that define you?" Sadie asked.

"No, no, no. It only defines *them*. I know that's not who I am. I never for one second think that's who I am. That's the difference, Sadie. You let them tell you who you are. And you buy it, hook, line, and sinker! I always keep myself, my real true self, to myself. I never compromise that. Ever. I never do anything I do not 100% want to do, and I never give in to their fantasies. If I did, I'd let Darien suck on my tit forever! I let him suck on me until it didn't work for me anymore. Then, he got kicked to the curb. I'm sure that did not fit in to his fantasy, but I don't give a shit. I am in everything for me, and only me."

Sadie could not help wondering where she fit in to Ella's world. How did her being there work for Ella? Not knowing how they had gotten to that point in the conversation, and feeling weary, she tried to get the story back on track. "So, Adam..."

Ella looked dazed and then refocused, "Yes,

Adam. So, Adam was different because I didn't have my normal defenses, and what was even stranger was that I didn't need them. In Iowa we kind of just fell into sleeping together pretty quickly, but when he came to Little Heart it was different. We spent days and nights together, wandering around the mountains, hanging out by the river, talking. We touched and kissed, but he did not seem too eager to sleep with me again. At night we talked and held each other and slept.

"By around the fourth day or so, we had gained a level of intimacy I had not ever known. Sex was always the opposite of intimacy to me; it was my defense against intimacy. But when we had gotten truly intimate, emotionally intimate I mean, the sex just came naturally. It was not about getting off, like it usually is for me, it was... well, spiritual, that's the only way I can describe it."

"What do you mean, *spiritual*?"

"I mean that it was no longer sex, it was something different. It was bonding or closeness, or... something. So, this one night, we're 'making love,' which was a term I always thought was just a euphemism, by the way, and it's dark and we have some candles lit and we're on some blankets on the floor. We're right in the middle of it, and all of a sudden he stops. I don't know if I can describe it, Sadie, it was the strangest thing. He stopped, and stood up. Then he knelt down and scooped me up. He just scooped me right up and held me against his chest. He just stood there, both of us totally nude, cradling me like a little baby in the dark in the middle of the room. I don't know what happened, Sadie, but I just started bawling. I cried and cried and he just held me against him, standing there totally silently in the dark."

Sadie was moved. "Wow," was all she could think of to say.

"Yeah, I know. Wow."

Sadie was afraid to ask, but now she really wanted to know: "So then what happened? You said it fell apart?"

"Oh, yeah, well, it was kind of inevitable. You can't really live life one way and then expect to turn a corner and live a totally different life. I mean, he figured out I was a drug dealer pretty quickly, but that didn't really seem to shock him or anything. He doesn't get high himself, but he didn't really judge me for it or anything. He realized it's my livelihood. It was the other stuff he couldn't forgive I guess. So he left."

"He just left?"

"Well, I went out one morning to go get orange juice and walk Kelpie, and I came back and he was gone. He had found the list of names and addresses, and the letters, the ones I had gotten back from my cross-country boys. I'm not very good at being secretive. They were in a box on my desk, not really hidden. He was probably looking for something, a pen or something. He found them. He left them out on the desk."

"Oh, shit."

"Yeah."

"Did you ever hear from him again?"

"No."

"Oh, Ella, I'm sorry," said Sadie. She was, really

sorry for her.

"Don't be. It's fine. It was a cool experience."

"But, I mean, don't you... don't you love him?"

"Oh, I don't know about that," said Ella brusquely. "I mean, he was awesome, really, really cool. I'm glad I spent that time with him, but I don't really know what love is."

"Well, it sounds like love to me," Sadie said.

"No offense, Sadie Dear, but I don't think you're the authority on the subject. No, I mean, I do feel a lot of regret about it."

"Well, don't you still have his address?" Sadie asked.

"Yeah, so?"

"Well, maybe you could write to him and explain."

"Explain what, that I'm sorry he found out that I tried to screw him over? There's really no way to justify that. The true explanation is not pretty, no matter how you try to dress it up."

"Yeah, but you could tell him you have feelings for him, that you didn't expect to, that you're sorry."

"I'm not sure if that's true. How would I tell him that the entire life I have led up until now is not really me, that the me he got to know in the week he was here was the real genuine me, but all the stuff I did before I knew him was just a distorted version of me. How would that go over?"

"Yeah, but didn't you say that you keep the true You to yourself? You let Adam see the true You, didn't you? So isn't all the rest irrelevant?" This seemed clear and simple to Sadie.

"Oh boy, Sadie. It's not that easy. The truth is, that week scared the shit out of me! Part of the way I keep my power is by keeping everyone at an arm's length. It was terrifying to have Adam slip into my circle, slip inside my world, where I am so used to being alone by myself, where I am comfortable by myself. I don't know if I could really *be* with someone. I don't know if I'll ever be able to really be with someone."

Sadie got up her courage, "So why do you trust me, then. I mean, I feel like you're telling me all this, so you must trust me."

"Sweet Sadie," said Ella. "You're like Kelpie. You could never hurt me, or anyone really, except yourself. I guess I trust you because I see how vulnerable you are, how much you let other people use you. I kind of resent you for it, but then I also want to see you fight back and get angry and get protective of yourself. That's probably why I tease you sometimes. I just want to see you fight harder."

"Maybe I need to fight more and you need to fight less," said Sadie.

"Ah, little grasshopper!" said Ella. "The student becomes the master!" They both laughed.

Sadie yawned again, and Ella snuck in and gave her a quick kiss next to her lips. "G'night, Sadie," she said.

"G'night, Ella." Ella turned off the kitchen and hall lights and closed the door to her room. Her bedroom light stayed on glowing from below her door. Sadie was suddenly wide awake. She lay in the dark, her face tingling where she had received Ella's kiss long into the night.

Chapter 6: Crosswords

Ella

Ella awoke to mottled sunlight filtering in through the window, making shifting patterns on the far wall across from her little cave. Kelpie lay next to her and sensing her wakening, nuzzled her face. She had gotten Kelpie as a puppy when she was nine. One of the women who came to give birth on the island had brought her Australian Kelpie with her, and the dog had given birth, too. Most of the pups went home with the mom, but Ella's mother had let her keep Kelpie. She must have felt bad for Ella, with so many transient visitors to the island, and so few children that stayed any length of time. Ella called the dog Kelpie, not only because of her breed, but because she had a habit of eating seaweed when she was a tiny puppy, running along the beach after Ella.

She had really missed her dog during the year she lived in the tower. Aurora had convinced Ella to let her take Kelpie with her when she first went to Oregon. Aurora loved Kelpie, too, and Ella was still unsure about where she was going to live. Ella regretted that decision the whole time they were apart. In addition to her business venture, one of the other main reasons for Ella's trip out West was to retrieve her dog. Since she returned from that trip, she had rarely been apart from Kelpie. Ella felt more connected to her dog than she did to most people.

It was still early. She had been up late after talking to Sadie, thinking about Adam. Even getting to bed so late, Ella's habit of rising early predominated. It was typical for her to wake up, take Kelpie out, and be home drinking her tea before any of her peers were even cracking their eyelids. She got dressed and quietly opened her bedroom door, not wanting to wake Sadie. She began to pass by the living room, but noticed that all the blankets were folded on the couch and Sadie was gone. Ella was a light sleeper, but had not even heard her leave. On the table next to the couch, a little note was pinned under the corner of her honey bear, and said simply:

"Ella: Thanks for the honey. –Sadie"

Ella chuckled. She threw her bomber jacket on and went out the door with Kelpie at her heels. Sometimes people gave her a hard time because she never put a leash on her, but when they saw that Kelpie never left her side, and would sit and wait outside any door Ella entered until she reappeared, they generally left her alone about it. She walked up to the field and looked at the hole in the sky where the tower used to be. The fire fighters had nailed big tarps over the top of the roof to cover the gaping opening. The sight of the missing tower wrenched her heart; it felt like a piece of her soul was gone. It was deeply unsettling to her that the one piece of Little Heart that she felt the most attached to had been destroyed. It felt too damn specific. It gave her the sense that someone was watching her, knew her inside and out, and was sending her a very important and painful message.

She played with Kelpie on the field in their traditional game of run and jump at me, run away in a big circle, then run and jump at me again. Then they headed back to Market Street. Approaching her door, Cooper was already standing there, 40 ounce of Olde English and New York Times under his arm. Cooper was in his mid-thirties, but looked much older with his severe cheekbones, ever downward pointing scowl, and scraggly hair. He'd always been ornery, but really earned the nickname of "Cranky" when his record store went under a year or so before. He took the opportunity to begin drinking round the clock, becoming belligerent to strangers and townies alike, blaming everyone for the demise of his business. Ella admired his disdain for convention, and recently he became one of the men Ella slept with. They ended up getting along so well that it had quickly fizzled into a platonic friendship.

Cooper did not even seem to notice or mind when she stopped having sex with him. He still came over in the mornings, drank his beer, did his crossword puzzle, and ranted about all of the crappy unsophisticated people in the town whose unquenchable thirst for mediocrity forced him to close Off Beat Records. Ella embraced Cooper's fierceness, and loved to see the sweet gentle tenderness that lurked right under the surface.

"Hey, Coop," Ella said.

Cooper turned around, his bony shoulders poking out of the old black suit jacket that he always wore. It had a striped lining, and its shabby formality evoked an aging professor. "Ella! There you are, I was wondering why I didn't hear Kelpie barking. Hey little Kelper, little Kelp-meister, Kelpie Girl! Such a good girl, don't let those killer bats get you!" he said, making a little bat out of his hand by sticking out his thumb and pinkie and making it swoop down to "attack" her. Kelpie loved Cooper, and loved playing "killer bats." She barked and twirled in circles to avoid/defend against the invading marauder. Cooper lived alone with two cats who also loved killer bats. His girlfriend and business partner of many years had left concurrent with the failure of the record store. While he had always had an irritable nature, that double injury had not done wonders for his temperament. Despite his disdain for humans, Cooper was always indulgent to four-legged creatures.

"C'mon in," said Ella, unlocking the door. Cooper walked in to the kitchen table, laying down his paper. He unscrewed the cap on his forty and took a big guzzle before even sitting down. "You want coffee?" she asked him.

"Sure, that will be a good chaser."

Ella started making the coffee. Cooper liked it strong and black. He started working on the crossword puzzle and had several answers completed by the time Ella joined him at the table. She saw him write "Elpis" and asked what it meant.

"Hope," he said. "It's Greek," he explained when he saw Ella's puzzled expression.

"Yeah, but how did you figure that out?"

"The clue said 'Hope' and I already had the "E" from "ether" and the "L" from "Lindbergh," so it really couldn't be anything else."

"Oh. So how did you just happen to know that?" asked Ella, not convinced that normal everyday people knew the Greek word for hope.

"It's basic Greek mythology- the last evil in Pandora's box."

"Hope? Hope was the last evil in Pandora's box? How is hope evil?" asked Ella.

"Well, *elpis* really has the connotation of expectant hope. The Greeks didn't really see hope as such a wonderful thing. It was viewed as part of suffering, like when you hope for something and it doesn't come to pass. That's kind of worse than not having hoped at all," he said.

"I guess," said Ella. "I still don't know how you knew that. I must have missed that class in school," she said.

"I took a class in mythology at Bryn Mawr," he explained.

"Bryn Mawr? That's a women's college!" Ella said. She had actually looked into applying there when she was first in high school.

"It is, but at the graduate level they take men, too," said Cooper. "I was one of the lucky devils, surrounded by smart, privileged girls, just looking for ways to rebel against their parents. I never graduated. I got too distracted helping one of those privileged girls rebel, followed her back to New York. That's how I ended up here."

"Oh, that was Tabitha," said Ella, figuring out that it was his ex.

"Yep. Tabitha, elpis, same thing. Shit'll get you every time," he mumbled.

He swilled his bottle and made a sizeable dent in the amount of liquid remaining and returned to quickly scratching letters in block print Across and Down. Ella watched, fascinated as he filled in the squares. Although she had seen him do this many times, it never ceased to awe her. Cooper worked steadily, pausing now and again to comment on the sad state of humanity. He finished the crossword and the bottle about the same time and pushed back the chair, lighting up a Marlboro.

"That was a great show last night," said Cooper with a rare grin.

"Yeah, I barely got to talk to you!" said Ella.

"We should have the Menace play here every week," he said. "Actually, we should have the new band that Raiche and I are forming play. It's called Carbon. We're both going to play guitar, it's going to be radical. We'll break eardrums all over Little Heart!"

"Sounds great, Coop," said Ella.

"Actually, maybe we'll play at Christmas time, we'll do it during their fucking Little Heart tree lighting ceremony, play it out the fucking window so that nobody can hear their "Silent Night." Fuck all of them! Sniveling shit-eaters, going to their shopping malls and buying their pre-fabricated lame-ass music, what's wrong with people? It disgusts me. This whole town disgusts me," Cooper took a big gulp of his coffee. Suddenly his expression changed, and he started laughing out loud.

"What?"

"I'm gonna show those fuckers. I know what I'm going to do, Ella. I'm going to sabotage their tree lighting! The night before, I'm going to sneak down to the park and fuck with the electricity. Then, when they're all gathered there, ready to light the tree, it just won't light! I'll leave a letter, telling them why their shitty tree doesn't even deserve to get lit and they can read that instead! I need some paper!" Ella gave him a note pad, and he started scribbling away.

Ella was used to Cooper's wild schemes. He had about one a day. They usually didn't amount to much. He'd rant and plot and then he'd move on to something else. Ella finished cleaning up from the night before, working around him as he sat with his hair hanging over his face, madly detailing his plan.

"Listen, Ella, listen to this: 'To All Ye Faithless Fuckers of Little Heart…'" he began. They were interrupted by a knock at the door and Kelpie's sharp voice announcing more visitors.

Ella opened the door and saw Hugh and Lilli standing there.

"Hey, Ella, howya doin?" Hugh said, big smile.

Lilli, little smile.

"Hey you two, c'mon in. Cooper's here," Ella said. They walked in to the kitchen and Cooper immediately swarmed in on Hugh, reading from his vendetta. Hugh jumped right in to it, suggesting words and laughing at the idea of all those happy townspeople showing up to light a tree and having it fail at the big moment.

"That's terrific, that'll show 'em," Hugh agreed. "Hey, Ella, can we buy a dime bag?"

"Sure." Ella hated selling dimes, but had a few customers who just couldn't scrape together enough for an eighth. It was better to sell them $10 worth of pot than front them a $25 bag and not get paid. She always separated out a few dimes for them.

She went and got the bag and Hugh gave her two crumpled fives. He took out some rolling papers and dumped the bag out on Cooper's completed crossword. He began separating out the seeds. He folded a paper in half, then half again, and sprinkled weed in the crease down the middle. Then he took another bag out of his pocket. It had a little dark brown ball in it, like a lump of clay. He broke off a piece and rolled it into a long snake, laying it across the weed before rolling it.

"What do you have there, Hugh, hash?" asked Ella.

"Yeah, from Rasta Ben," said Hugh. "We've been smoking it since Tuesday, right Lilli?" Lilli nodded. Ella noticed the red rims around her eyes.

"I don't know, you guys, I wouldn't really fuck with that too much. Don't you know you shouldn't buy drugs from a White guy who calls himself a Rasta?" Ella laughed.

"Don't worry, Ella. He's no competition. Nobody has weed like you. I like hash, it's strong, makes you trip out," said Hugh.

"Exactly, that's the problem. Weed is supposed to mellow you out, not make you wacky. Hash is pretty toxic. It's made out of the resin of all kinds of crappy pot and shake that nobody would ever buy," said Ella.

"I like it," Hugh repeated and finished rolling. He took out a lighter and lit up. He knew Ella well enough by now to know it was okay to smoke in her kitchen. He didn't even bother offering it to Cooper, who was a steadfast drinker but did not smoke pot, handing it instead to Ella. Ella waved it away, so he passed it instead to Lilli. Looking like a glazed donut, Lilli focused on the joint as she inhaled, making her eyes go crosswise, then handed it back to Hugh. They passed it back and forth, the smoke filling the kitchen. Ella didn't like the smell of the resinous hashish, and worried a little about Lilli, who looked more and more like an empty shell.

"Hey, Lilli, you want some tea?" Ella asked. Tea was her solution for everything.

"Sure, thanks," said Lilli. Ella put a pot on and began to root around in her little paper bags and bottles of herbs for a specific one.

"I'll take some coffee," said Hugh.

"Help yourself," said Ella, gesturing toward the pot.

"Nothing better than hash and coffee in the morning," said Hugh as he poured himself a cup.

Cooper was still writing away. "Okay, listen to this: '...So, in conclusion, all Ye Good Fuckers of Little Heart, you do not deserve the light, since you will never experience the glimmering light of charity in your soul that would herein be represented by the lights on this tree. The wholesomeness and goodness that are supposed to be the hallmarks of the holiday season will never be possessed by you, Fuckers, and so therefore, I pronounce that since you will never have the eternal lights of forgiveness and generosity, may you live forever in the dark where you belong!'"

"Bravo! Bravo!" clapped Hugh, and Cooper stood up to take a deep bow. "That'll show those Fuckers, Coop!" Hugh said.

Lilli mustered a mediocre smile, but Ella was not convinced that she had even been following the conversation. "So, Lilli, what are you doing today?" inquired Ella, trying to rouse her from her apparent stupor.

"Huh? Oh, uh, not much," responded Lilli.

"Yeah, we'll probably go down to Raymond's house," Hugh interjected. "We have some recording to do, we're working on this new series of 'sound paintings'," he said.

"Cool," said Ella, wondering how Lilli was going to make it through the day, and imagining her, blindly following Hugh wherever he went, listening to 'sound paintings' or whatever else he concocted through a hashish haze. Hugh might have the constitution for smoking hash first thing in the morning, but she could tell that Lilli did not. She poured a cup of tea and set it in front of Lilli.

"Thanks," said Lilli and put her hands around the outside of the cup, staring into the liquid.

"Yeah, we're really doing some experimental shit," Hugh went on. "We'll record a noise like a door squeaking or a dog barking and distort it until you can't recognize it, then put layers of guitar, drum tracks, paint in different melodies, so it will sound like a gypsy caravan one minute and then blend in to a sad country western, then a jazz ensemble."

"Cool," Ella said again.

"You guys should let me play guitar, I've got these rad licks I've worked out, very industrial, they'd fit right in," said Cooper.

"Yeah, that would be great! You should come down with us, you can use Raymond's guitar," Hugh said.

"No, no, no, I'd need to go home and get my baby," said Cooper. "Playing another man's guitar is like playing another man's woman. I'll swing by my place first!"

They rustled around, getting their coats on, gathering up their belongings and planning their recording session.

"Thanks, Ella," said Hugh.

"See you tomorrow, Ella," said Cooper.

"Bye, Ella. Thanks for the tea, I mean... Sorry, thanks anyway," said Lilli.

Kelpie accompanied the trio to the door and then trotted back to Ella, looking up expectantly. Ella sighed as she looked over her kitchen table. On Cooper's side was an empty forty, a crumpled Marlboro pack, and the forgotten Manifesto. At

Hugh's chair was the crossword puzzle with a small pile of seeds. At Lilli's seat was a full cup of tea, still steaming and untouched.

♦ ♦ ♦

Ella took a beige phone out from her kitchen drawer and unwound the long curly cord that was wrapped around it. She plugged it in to an inconspicuous little hole in the wall. Picking up the receiver, she heard a dial tone. Ella did not technically have phone service, but for some reason the line was tied in to the apartment next door. The frat boys who lived there didn't mind if she sometimes plugged in her phone to make calls. When the phone bill came, they brought it over and she paid for any long distance calls she had made and toked them up. They didn't mind at all.

She dialed Aurora's number. It rang a few times and then Aurora's sleepy voice answered.

"Hey, Sis," said Ella.

"Ella… it's early," said Aurora. Ella had forgotten the time difference.

"Sorry, good morning! Hey, aren't you farmers? Farmers are supposed to get up early," Ella joked.

"Not farmers who stay up all night packaging produce and enjoying the bounties of their harvest."

"How is the harvest?"

"Beautiful, beautiful," said Aurora. "Purple, sticky, we're getting better and better. You know what does it? Coffee grounds. We go to the local café and get all their discarded grounds."

"How's your husband?"

"Ha, ha. He's great, he's one hell of a farmer, if only he didn't SNORE SO LOUD!" She was obviously still in bed with her beau.

"Did you get the letter I sent from your mom with the last money order?"

"Yeah, I wrote back, you should get it in a few days, along with a package of "socks" from Granny."

"Granny sure does send me a lot of socks," laughed Ella. It was a growing joke between them based on the conversations Ella had with the lady at the post office. Aurora always sent her packages addressed from Granny Green, and Ella always chatted away with the post office attendant about Granny Green, who apparently thought Ella was freezing out here in the far East, always sending her those darn socks and blankets she knits herself.

"How's my baby?" asked Aurora.

"She's right here, want to talk to her? C'mere, Kelpie girl, talk to Aurora." She held the receiver out and Kelpie tilted her head to the sound of Aurora's voice on the other end and let out a loud yip.

"She misses you. I miss you, too, Sis," said Ella.

"Are you okay?" asked Aurora. Ella wasn't usually sentimental.

"Of course. I'm fine. Just… Ror, do you think I'm like a man?"

"What are you talking about?"

"I mean, do you think I use men the way men use women?"

"Of course you do. You always have. Remember the boys in high school? You had them wrapped around your fingers. Breaking hearts left and right. But at least you got them high when you dumped them. Softened the blow."

"I'm serious, though."

"Why? It's never bothered you before." She was right.

"I just wonder, is it okay? I always thought it was fine, since men do it all the time and never give two shits about how it affects women. I never really cared, I felt like it evened the playing field. Now, I don't know. Just because men do it to women, does it mean it's okay to do it back to them?"

"Yeah, but you're kind of like a guerilla soldier on the side of women, Ella. You're fighting back for all of us girls who have gotten trashed by men. I always saw it as... how do you call it?...poetic justice. At least one chick in Little Heart is not getting hurt," said Aurora. She was more than familiar with the toxicity that the town held for young women.

"I guess," said Ella. There was a click on the line and some fumbling. "Hey, who's there?"

"Huh? Oh, hey Ella, it's me, Boot. Great party last night! Gotta call my mom. It's her birthday." Frat boy. Boot had gotten his nickname from his bar trick of drinking out of his boot when drunk.

"Sorry, man, just getting off the phone with my sister. Goodbye Aurora!"

"Adios, mi Hermana, te amo," said Aurora.

"Te amo."

"And, Sis, don't let those Fuckers bother you. You're fine. You've always been fine," said Aurora.

Ella hung up and unplugged the phone, bundled up the phone cord, and put it back in the drawer. She put on another pot of water. There was a knock at the door. She opened it and saw Seth. Number three.

"Hey, man," she said.

"Hey," he said and stepped in, touching her face and kissing her next to her ear. Ella backed away, ducking under his arm.

"Got the kettle on," she explained. He followed her into the kitchen.

"I heard you had a party here last night. How come I wasn't invited?" asked Seth.

"It was a keg party, Seth, everybody's invited."

"Yeah, but you didn't tell me about it."

"There were posters all over town. I didn't realize you needed a personal invitation." Seth was in his twenties. He was cute in a serial killer type of way, skinny with tattoos and a shaved head. He had been around the town for a while and had a face that Aurora used to joke looked like a snake. He had rings in both ears and snaggly teeth that Ella used to find sexy. He was a lot cuter when he was just a hardened street dealer to her. He mostly sold acid, but dabbled in cocaine and even heroin occasionally. "Which reminds me," she said, "can you bring this thing back uptown for me? It needs to go back to the beverage outlet," she pointed with her foot to the empty keg in the corner.

"Sure, I'll take it with me when I leave."

"You want some tea, or coffee?" she asked.

"Coffee would be great," he said.

"There it is," Ella pointed. "It's not really fresh."

Seth began to pour himself a cup. "What's up with you, Ella? I thought you liked me?"

"I do like you," she lied.

"I know you've been sleeping with that kid with the mohawk."

"So?"

"So, I really like you. I thought you liked me."

"I do, so what does that have to do with anything?"

"Well, I just don't really like to share. I really care about you. I was hoping we could be, you know... together."

Ella almost laughed. "You mean, like a couple?"

"Yeah, well, I mean, don't you have any feelings for me at all?"

"What do you mean?"

"I mean, I'm not a toy, Ella," she could tell he was really hurt, and felt a twinge of guilt.

"Look, Seth, I do like you. You were a great friend before we started sleeping together, and I want to be your friend. Can we do that? Can we be friends?"

"Are you kidding me? You're giving me the 'can we be friends' routine?"

"Look, I don't want to hurt you. I think we just had different ideas about this. I thought you were like me, just wanting to have some fun," she was confused at how they had gotten here, from the aerobic fucking they had been doing for the past few weeks to this emotional place in her kitchen. It was more than she had bargained for.

"I did want to have fun. I had fun. I just thought it might be more than that."

"I don't really understand what that means, 'more than that,'" Ella confessed.

"That's obvious. Look, forget it. Forget I mentioned it," said Seth. He took one sip of his coffee and then dumped it down the sink.

"Okay."

"I gotta go. I'll see you later," he said.

"Later," said Ella. Seth walked toward the door. "Wait, Seth!" He turned around, hopeful. "The keg," she reminded him. His face dropped. She wanted him to say, "Fuck you, Ella, and fuck your keg," but instead, he sighed, shook his head, and walked back and hauled up the keg. She held the door for him on the way out.

His shoulder bumped hers. "Sorry," he said, a gentleman to the end, despite the tattoos.

"Yeah, me too."

Chapter 7: Security Blanket

Lilli

Lilli trudged behind Hugh and Cooper. They spoke animatedly to one another about music while she followed, focusing on their backs and the ground. At one point, Hugh seemed to remember that she was there, smiled back at her and reached out his hand. She sped up to grab his hand, but he just squeezed it and let go again, and continued his conversation with Cooper. This made the whole trip worth it to Lilli, though, and after that she did not mind following, even though her body felt like gel. All she really wanted was to lie down somewhere. The hash seemed to add to Hugh's abundance of energy, but it overloaded Lilli and made her want to just sit in a corner and shut down.

They had accompanied Cooper down Chapel

Street to get his guitar, then went the back way down by the river and the old stone houses to Raymond's house. He lived on Lock Street, before the bridge by the abandoned railroad tracks, in a little house tucked into the side of the road. Lilli thought he was so lucky to live in that house, with really nice hippie roommates who seemed to all enjoy each other and even cooked together. Raymond had been Lilli's friend. For years going back they would hang out and party together and even had accidentally slept together once after a long night of drinking. They had remained friends, despite this slip up, and when Hugh met him, he and Hugh hit it off. They started playing and recording together, and Hugh found a companion in him who was as eager to be liked as he was.

Raymond even liked to party the same, and because he had a regular job during the week, working in the fish market, he had money to spend. Although he bathed meticulously, rare in Little Heart, he could never quite get rid of the light aroma of fish. Lilli liked Raymond. She considered him a good friend and felt very comfortable around him, like he was not judging her. A natural salesman, Raymond was carefully polite and friendly to everyone. He blended in with every crowd due to his generous nature, but was not entirely accepted by the punks for his clean look, button-down shirts, and jeans with- god forbid- no rips or holes.

"Hey Lil," he greeted her when they arrived at his house. They walked through the strange dark empty living room that nobody in the house ever used into the kitchen and past to Raymond's room. It was always neat, like the rest of him. His bed, a futon on a frame, was folded up carefully into a couch during the day. Lilli took off her shoes and curled up in a corner of it. "Guess what I got?" said Raymond. He took out a bag of shriveled gray things.

"Shrooms!" said Hugh excitedly. "I haven't done those in years!" Raymond handed him the bag and Hugh picked out a few choice pieces and passed it to Lilli. Lilli had done mushrooms once the year before and had a very bad trip. This was apparently not enough to keep her from trying again. It had always been Lilli's problem that she could never seem to pass up any kind of drug that was handed to her. Even if she did not go specifically looking for it, if it was offered to her, she had never been able to say no. She took out two small stems and a cap, thinking this was modest, and popping them into her mouth, passed back the bag.

"None for me! I don't touch that shit," said Cooper, who had stopped at the deli when they left Ella's to pick up his second forty of the day, although it was still well before noon. Hugh had gotten two tall boys and handed one to Lilli now. Lilli cracked it and took a long sip, rinsing the pungent earthy taste of the mushrooms down. It seemed to quench a thirst she didn't even realize she'd had, and for a moment, Lilli remembered the cup of tea she had left on Ella's table. She took another long sip, and felt her nerves begin to settle.

Coop, Hugh, and Raymond quickly got to work, setting up their equipment, chattering about the project, and laughing. Lilli was forgotten, but didn't really mind. She settled on to the warm blanket that covered the futon. She was really okay with being an observer of the action. She liked seeing Hugh happy and involved, and among friends. Being included in that was fulfilling to her. Since being with Hugh, she had sat in countless rehearsals, recording sessions, and had even sat with him in his intense hours of solo work. Having been lonely for so long, just being part of a couple meant a tremendous deal to her. Hugh never ran out of energy or ideas, so she never really had to think about what they were going to do. He made all the plans and decisions, and Lilli was content to follow along and just be there with him on whatever adventure he selected.

"Hey, Lil, you want another beer?" Raymond asked. She hadn't even realized she had finished hers. She had been sipping it and liked the taste and the slurping sound it made going into her mouth, so she just kept sipping until the can was totally empty. She had been holding the empty can, staring straight into the hole for some time without realizing it, feeling as if she was inside the dark and cavernous interior.

"Uh, yeah, thanks," she said. Her skin felt all wobbly.

Raymond returned with a Heineken and handed it to her. She liked the difference between the heavy bottle in one hand and the light can in the other. "Want me to take that?" asked Raymond.

Lilli looked at him, but couldn't figure out what to do. Finally, she realized he was talking about the empty can and handed that to him hesitantly, still unsure if she was doing the right thing. He grinned at her. She grinned back. He started laughing and she started laughing, too.

"Yeah, you guys are starting to get off, aren't you?" asked Hugh. "I'm feeling it, too. Hey, Raymond, where's your bong? I want to smoke a little hash." Raymond got up to get the bong for Hugh, and Lilli got fascinated with the colors on the blanket, red and orange geometric shapes, tracing them with her fingers. She pulled the blanket up off the futon and over her, up to her chin, liking the scratchy wool against her skin. She listened to the bubbling of the bong as Hugh smoked, then handed the bong to Raymond. He smoked and handed it to Lilli. Lilli felt immobilized, with the blanket wrapped up to her chin.

"Do you want any?" asked Raymond. Lilli nodded and so Raymond held the bong to her lips and lit it for her. She inhaled deeply, but didn't anticipate how much smoke she pulled in and hacked, coughing repeatedly in a huge puff of smoke. Her throat and lungs stung, and she imagined little microscopic shards of glass sticking her up and down her esophagus. Hugh and Raymond laughed and Lilli started laughing again, making it hurt even more. Raymond handed her the beer she had set down on the table next to her and she took it and drank deeply.

Cooper and Hugh still fumbled with equipment, talking and tinkering. Raymond sat down on the futon next to Lilli. He took the other end of the blanket she had pulled over her and pulled it up to his chin, too. It covered his shoulders with just his head popping out. As Lilli watched him, mesmerized, Raymond sunk lower and lower down into the blanket until just his eyes peeked out over the top. His eyes looked very black and bounced from left to right, like a cartoon character, and then his face emerged again, a big wide smile plastered on. He did this a few times, sinking down into the blanket, and then slowly re-emerging back over the edge, smiling and moving his eyes back and forth. It gave Lilli the impression of some kind of Mexican puppet or jack-in-the-box, wrapped in the colorful blanket, expression frozen except for his eyes, and moving up and down, as if operated by someone else.

At first it was funny, but it started to have an eerier and eerier impact on Lilli. Raymond's frozen smile began to seem possessed and sinister. It didn't help that Cooper and Hugh had started playing, and Coop's guitar was railing a frenetic discordant solo while Hugh adjusted and distorted the sound. Hugh began accompanying on keyboard, a melody like a spooky carnival ride. Lilli started to panic and felt her heart beating. She became very pre-occupied with trying to breathe and swallow, this being alarmingly hard to figure out and coordinate. She put her hand to her throat to try to guide this process from the outside, but was even more unsettled to feel a strange inflated vein in her neck where her chin met her throat. She traced the outline of the bump to make sure her fingers weren't playing tricks on her, and determined that there was definitely a pronounced lump there.

What could it be? Was this a normal part of her neck? No, definitely not. She felt it some more, and had a terrifying revelation. It was cancer, it must be. She was sure. Thoroughly freaking out inside now, she tried not to totally lose it. She surreptitiously continued to stroke and touch the lump, her distress increasing by the minute. Raymond had gotten distracted with something in the corner, and she was glad he was not doing the evil puppet trick anymore. Still, her dread built as she felt the bump and could almost feel the cancer beginning to grow and devour her from the inside. Then she worried that maybe she was making it spread by touching it too much, and pulled her hand away. She needed to do something, fast. This was an emergency.

She sat in crisis and internal turmoil for what seemed like another hour as the boys played, unsure of what to do. Raymond joined in and began playing his guitar as well. Finally, she got up the nerve to interrupt the music to talk to Hugh. Making her body cooperate to stand and mobilize toward him took incredible concentration and Lilli felt like she was moving through iron. Finally, she made it over and then had to figure out how to make her mouth move to speak into his ear. He leaned toward her, but over the music couldn't hear the disjointed syllables she was trying to connect and force out of her mouth. Finally, he shushed the other guys and asked Lilli what was wrong.

"I need... to talk to you... outside," she was able to get out. Hugh looked concerned and stood up. They went out the door in Raymond's bedroom that let out to the street. Somehow, it was getting dark and the streetlights were on. Wasn't it just noon?

"What's the matter?" Hugh asked when the door was closed.

"I think something's wrong with me," said Lilli, not sure how to explain her concerns.

"What?"

"I don't know, I think... I have a bump in my neck," said Lilli. She lifted her chin up and indicated the location of the scary object beneath her skin.

Hugh looked very serious and looked at her neck closely, then touched it. He stroked it and looked really hard at where Lilli was showing him.

"It's nothing, Lil. There's nothing there. I don't see anything," he said.

"But does it feel like anything?" she asked, unconvinced.

Hugh carefully felt along Lilli's neck. "There's nothing there. It's perfectly normal, Lilli. It's just your neck."

Lilli was not sure, but felt her neck again. This time, it just felt like her neck, smooth, with the bumps and ridges of a normal neckline. She let out her breath and relief swelled over her. "Shit, Hugh, I think I'm really fucked up," she said. "I thought I was dying."

Hugh smiled at her and drew her close. "You're

okay, you're just tripping out."

Of course! He was right. She was just tripping out. Her heart welled with love and gratitude for him. He was so smart, so in control. He always knew exactly what to do. She was so lucky to have him! She hugged him tightly. He kissed her on the forehead and she felt so nurtured, so looked after, that she almost overflowed with joy. They went back inside to Cooper and Raymond, who were engaged in a cacophonous musical exchange.

The rest of the evening passed with no further incident. Lilli was even able to pass up the hash bong that was passed her way, realizing that this did not help her to remain self-composed. Instead, she invested in the medicinal calm of a few more Heinekens and smoked a joint later with Hugh and Cooper, once she began to come down enough to feel like she was going to survive the bad trip. She was awash with relief, and promised herself she would never do mushrooms again.

Coming down, and getting a little drowsy and tipsy from the beers, she sat on the futon, leaning her head against the arm of the frame. She watched Hugh as he played his bass. He looked right up at her and into her eyes after every change, intent and purposeful. She smiled a relaxed and happy smile, looking back at him, waiting each time he glanced down for his eyes to bounce back up and meet hers again. She felt completely at peace, knowing that this was exactly where she belonged in the universe, at the other end of Hugh's gaze.

♦ ♦ ♦

The next day was Sunday and they slept in until late in the afternoon. They had not left Raymond's until the sun was coming up, walking back to their apartment holding hands the whole way. They crashed after making love, still a little zingy from the residual drugs in their systems. Lilli awoke to knocking on the apartment door. She went to open it and was surprised to find Finn there.

"Hey, Lil. You're still sleeping?" she asked.

"Yeah, we were up late at Raymond's. He and Hugh were recording. We didn't get to sleep until the morning."

"You look like shit," she said in typical Finn fashion.

"Thanks."

"Want to go get a cup of coffee?"

"Uh, okay, if you don't mind being seen with me. Where's Kairo?"

"Mom took him and Josey to some kids' movement class or something. I went to my meeting already. I was going to go home, but they won't be back for a while, so I decided to stop by and say 'hi' first."

"Oh, okay. Let me get dressed." Lilli went to her room and threw on some clothes and shoes. She came out to find Finn in the kitchen, looking over the empty beer cans stacked in their cases, overflowing cigarette trays, and bong sitting out on the table.

"It's not mine," said Lilli.

"I'm not the police."

They went down the stairs to the door that led to the street and walked down to the Gayfeather.

"Hey, Lilli! Oh, hi Finn!" It was Ella, waving from across the street, heading back up to her apartment with Kelpie. Finn and Lilli waved.

"Was that Ella?" asked Finn.

"Yeah," said Lilli.

"Wow, I haven't seen her since she was a little kid."

"Oh, that's right. I forgot that Mom is friends with her mom," said Lilli. It was a vague recollection from her pre-teen years, Ella coming with her mother to a potluck or two at their house, a quiet girl who dressed funny and read in the corner.

"Where does she live?" asked Finn.

"Above the pizza place. Right across from my apartment."

"That's my old apartment!" said Finn, surprised.

"Oh yeah, I forgot that you lived on Market Street when you first moved out. It's weird that it's the same place. That was so long ago."'

"Yeah, it was." They walked into the Gayfeather and sat at a booth. "I sold a lot of weed in that apartment," said Finn almost wistfully.

"Really?" said Lilli. "Huh. Interesting,"

"What is?"

"Oh, nothing, just that you sold weed. I didn't know that," said Lilli.

"Yeah, I did a lot of things I'm not proud of," said Finn.

Lilli was still tired, and a little cranky, and sensed a lecture coming on, or a long soliloquy on how Finn had transformed her life, the error of her old ways, and the benefits of her newfound sobriety. She didn't really have the stomach for it. "How's Mom?" she asked.

"Oh, she's... Mom. You know. All over the place. Saving the whales, and the trees, and whatever indigenous population is having an uprising somewhere, and fighting for equal rights for immigrants and flying squirrels. You know... Mom."

Lilli laughed, "Yeah, that's Mom."

The waitress came and they ordered coffee. Lilli got a breakfast special, even though it was three in the afternoon. She sat there stirring milk in her coffee, wanting to add sugar, but feeling like she'd be cheating on Hugh if she did. Finn stirred her own coffee for much longer than was necessary. Lilli had a moment of dread, and realized that they really had nothing to say to each other. "How's school?" Lilli asked. It seemed like a neutral topic.

"Oh, it's great. I'm doing really well. You know, I thought I was stupid. I've been out of school for so long, and I never finished high school, so I really didn't think I could do it. Now that I'm not getting high and drinking anymore, I have all this extra time. I'm reading and writing papers, I actually wish they'd move faster. In my English 101 class they assigned a story to read two weeks in advance. I finished it the first night and then had to wait two weeks to talk about it in class!"

"Wow," said Lilli dryly.

"Yeah, I know. It's pretty easy. I don't know what I was so scared about. You should really sign up to take your G.E.D., Lilli. It's really not so hard."

"No thanks," said Lilli. "I don't really buy into all that stuff."

"What stuff, education?"

"Just that there is anything special about taking some test. I don't need to prove anything. I've learned more since I've been out of school than I ever learned in it. Aside from basic math and reading, I've never used anything I learned in school."

"Well, I don't know about you, but when I was a dropout, I mean, before I got my G.E.D., it was always in the back of my mind, that I wasn't good enough, that I was a failure," said Finn. "It took me eight years to go back, and for all of those eight years it nagged at me."

"Well, I'm not like that," said Lilli. "I could care less about it, and I don't think it makes me less of a person. It's never bothered me." This was actually true. Almost none of Lilli's friends had completed high school. Hugh had graduated and had even taken some college classes, but most of the other people she knew, aside from the few students in the scene, never finished high school and many were working and making money regardless. The pinnacle of success in Little Heart was to get a job as a bartender or a cashier at one of the shops or in one of the restaurants as a waitress or line cook. The most common career path of the older punks was working in the tie dye factory and most of them had worked there at one point or another. Since Lilli never really thought beyond Little Heart, getting a high school diploma seemed irrelevant.

"I just think you'll regret it in the future, that's all," said Finn. You may want to do something else, move somewhere, become something other than a street urchin," said Finn.

This was a completely foreign concept to Lilli. "No, not really," said Lilli flatly.

"Oh...kay... Well, I can see I'm not getting anywhere."

Lilli had a flash memory of being fourteen. She had been so lonely that she had answered an ad in the *Village Voice* from an older artist in the city who was looking for a "petite" companion. They wrote back and forth a bit, and then Lilli had finally admitted how old she really was. Apparently, he was still curious, so he came up from the city to meet her anyway, and they had gone to the Gayfeather. He was much older, graying with a beard, even older than the "older" guys Lilli sometimes slept with when she was drunk. He was very polite, took her out to eat, and lectured her on picking directions in her life.

Being stark cold sober and feeling like she was out with her dad, as well as getting some weird looks from some of her friends who were around that day, Lilli barely spoke and couldn't wait for the "date" to be over. It was hellish. He left afterward and they never corresponded again. This felt like that: a bad interview, a total disconnect, an unwanted diatribe. She was back in the Gayfeather again, having a tortured conversation with someone who just wanted to give her an oratory on how she should live her life. "I'm not sure why you always feel like you need to lecture me, Finn."

"Well, you're my sister! I see the kind of lifestyle

you're living and it worries me. I used to live on Market Street, too, so believe me, I understand. It's just that there's a whole big world outside of Little Heart, and eventually, you may want to explore it."

This was unimaginable to Lilli. She knew that people went other places, like Raiche going to Europe on tour or when Ella went cross-country, but she could not seem to extend this concept to herself. Little Heart and Market Street were her whole world. In fact, a few years earlier when she had lived outside of town with her mom, she would lie awake at night and crave being on Market Street, just being there, even if nobody was around. She yearned for it, would have loved to just curl up under a street light and sleep straight on the street if she could. Once she took a trip to Rhode Island with her mother, who was trying to bond with her. Her mom had even left Josey with Finn for the week. Lilli was miserable. All she wanted to do was get back to Market Street. They ended up leaving and going home early. "This may be hard for you to believe, Finn, but I really like it here."

"No, it's not hard for me to believe. I lived on Market Street for years. I remember. I liked it, too. I liked it because it was easy. I didn't have to try too hard and nobody expected me to be any better than I was. The bar was set pretty low. Success was scoring a bag or getting someone to buy me beer."

"You really don't understand. There are a lot of talented people in Little Heart. Artists and musicians. Maybe they don't buy in to the idea that you have to get a degree and wear a suit and tie and work 40 hours a week, but that doesn't mean they're not successful," Lilli was mad. Finn was always projecting her tiresome values onto her. Next time she would decline an invitation to hang out with her.

"Yeah but what are they gonna do when they need to support a family, or need to get their teeth fixed, or if they want to buy a house?" Finn asked.

Lilli thought of all of the musicians she knew in their thirties, working at the bars or in construction, and playing in their bands in their time off. They seemed to be doing just fine. None of them had kids or owned houses, and Lilli had no idea what they did if they needed dental work. "They do just fine, Finn. They figure it out. Not everybody is you. You decided to have a baby. You have more responsibility because of that. That doesn't mean everyone else is a slacker."

Finn sighed. "You're right. I need to just keep the focus on me. It doesn't matter what anyone else is doing."

Lilli was puzzled. It was almost as if Finn were agreeing with her.

Finn continued, "My sponsor tells me the same thing. I get too worked up about what everyone else is doing, worrying that you'll go down the same path, get hurt. I need to just focus on fixing me now."

Lilli was speechless.

"This town was really bad for me, Lilli. The bars, the stagnation. Nobody expects you to do anything other than party. It's socially acceptable here to just get high and drink and zone out. You can pass years like that. I did."

"Yeah, but what else am I supposed to do? Live with mom, go to school? It's just not me, Finn. I hated that shit. I couldn't wait to get out. I saw all of the good Little Heart girls, getting good grades, looking into colleges, thinking about careers. That was just never me. I wanted to be on Market Street hanging out with my friends."

"I know, Lil, I really know. I was the same."

Lilli felt like Finn was actually being genuine for once, not talking down to her and acting superior as usual. "Hey, I know you're just worried about me, but I'm fine," she said.

"Okay," Finn said. "I'll just have to trust that you have your own path. I have enough work to do worrying about myself."

"Okay," said Lilli. "And Finn, it's really great that you're doing what you're doing. Going to school, getting your life together. I know it's good for you, and for Kairo."

"Thank you, Lilli," she said. "Kairo needs me to get it together. You're right. You only have yourself. I have Kairo. That was my choice and I have to do it the best I can and that means doing things differently than I used to. I'll try to leave you alone about your decisions. It's really none of my business. I do care about you, though, Lil, and I want you to know that if you ever need me, if it's ever not okay anymore, I'm here to talk to about it. I really will understand."

"Thanks, Finn," said Lilli. She was confident that she would never need or want to confide in Finn, but she did appreciate the sentiment.

Outside of the Gayfeather, Finn hugged Lilli goodbye. As she walked away, Maddock, a local character who had been a regular fixture on the corner of Market and Chapel Streets for decades, waved to Finn. Finn went over and gave him a hug and talked to him for a second, then went on her way. Maddock looked after her. Lilli approached him. Maddock was tall, with stringy gray hair, and always wore a flat leather cowboy hat. He had cerebral palsy and moved awkwardly, but worked every day, slowly cleaning the windows at the Gayfeather or sweeping the sidewalk in front. Mostly he just stood on the corner with his arms resting on the top of his broom, with his cart of implements tied all over with objects and bandanas, nearby. Lilli had met him when she was a kid. Her mom would sometimes give him rides to his house on the way to the mountain. He didn't drive and hitched rides every day to and from the street. His house was an old, run-down shack with pieces patched together, kind of like his clothing. Even in the summer, he wore a buttoned up denim shirt with belts covered with silver bangles crisscrossed over his chest in an "X".

"Hi, Maddock," she said walking up to him. He was stirred from watching Finn walk away.

"Hi!" he smiled his typical huge smile upon seeing Lilli.

"You've known my sister for a long time, huh?"

"Oh, yeah! That's your sister! I've known her since she was really young," he said. "She's still so beautiful!" Lilli struggled to understand Maddock through his strained and garbled speech, but she had no trouble hearing that.

"Yeah, Finn's always gotten a lot of attention for her looks," said Lilli.

"Like a queen!" said Maddock.

"Yeah, hey listen Maddock, have a good day!" said Lilli.

"Bye, Little Sis," said Maddock, laughing good-naturedly.

Lilli walked away feeling miffed, her good feelings toward Finn dissolving.

Back in her apartment, Hugh was in the kitchen making coffee, a towel around his waist. "Hey, you're up!" said Lilli.

"Yeah, just got out of the shower. Where'd you go?" he asked.

"I had breakfast with Finn. Breakfast, and it's almost dinner time!"

"Oh, good. How's Finnian?"

"Fine. You know, preaching the rapture, the regular," she said.

Hugh laughed. "She's really into those meetings now, isn't she?"

"Yeah, hey, did you know she used to sell weed?"

"Of course, everyone knows that. Come to think of it, she used to live in Ella's old apartment. Funny, must have weed-dealer karma in that place or something."

"Did you ever buy weed from her?"

"Uh... yeah. A few times," said Hugh, looking a little uncomfortable and becoming very intent on cleaning the few items in the sink.

"That's so weird," said Lilli. "You never told me

that."

"I figured you knew her history, but I guess you were just of a little kid back then."

"I knew you knew her from those days, but I didn't know you *knew* her, like hung out with her. Did you... hang out with her?"

"Not... really. I mean, we were always in the same circle. Coffee's ready! You want a cup?"

"Yeah, I could use another cup. Did you ever think she was beautiful?"

"Who, Finn? Uh, yeah, she's pretty unusual looking."

"But, beautiful?"

"Um... yeah. She's always been pretty striking. It's hard not to notice that."

"Oh." Lilli felt her heart sink a little dip.

"I mean, she's not like you, with your big blue eyes and sexy little body," he took the opportunity to give her a squeeze. "She's just always been very unique-looking. Some guys like that."

Lilli decided to accept that. Hugh plunked two cups of coffee on the table and she sat down with him.

"Why, does it bother you? You're not jealous of her, are you?" asked Hugh.

"No! It's just that people have been telling me how beautiful Finn is for my whole life. It gets annoying."

"I can understand that. My brother always got attention for being a jock. He was into sports, classically good-looking...popular. I always felt overshadowed by him."

Lilli breathed a sigh of relief. Once again, Hugh

knew what to say. He was just like her. It was why she connected so much to him. He had been bumped around, rejected, overlooked, like her.

"Don't worry, Lil, nobody can hold a candle to you," he said. She went over and sat on his lap. He held her in his strong arms, nuzzled her and kissed her, and for a minute, she remembered who she was.

Chapter 8: Smokescreen

Finn

Finn drove down her driveway and walked up the sidewalk to her empty trailer. She got anxious when she didn't have a schedule. It was one thing she had realized in the six months she'd been clean. If she had something to do, somewhere to be, she was able to push aside her ragged nerves that nagged beneath the surface. She made coffee at some of the meetings. That gave her a purpose and a task that could easily be accomplished.

Going to school helped, too, because there were so many deadlines, classes to attend, boxes to check, forms to complete. She could do that. It was the more subtle things, like filling an hour without Kairo, which were particularly hard. She had classes the next day, but had done all of her homework Friday night. Usually she called Janie when she didn't know what to do, but she had just left her at the meeting earlier, and for a change wanted to try to not bother her ten times a day.

Walking up the steps to her dark trailer, she reflected on how a few months ago she would have loved the chance to be alone to smoke a little before her mom came back with the kids. She walked in and put the teakettle on. It was probably a mistake having coffee with Lilli. She was having enough trouble sleeping, and she had coffee at the meeting, too. She used to do a bong hit or two before crashing at night when she was not out drinking. Since getting clean, she'd struggled with insomnia without her nighttime sedative. It was particularly hard after some of the later meetings she attended during the week when she had a few cups of coffee. It never occurred to her to just not drink coffee at the meetings.

Janie told her she was so used to self-medicating that she wanted to take a drug any time she had a normal emotion. If she was feeling something, she looked for something to ameliorate the feeling. Guiltily, she poured hot water over some roots she had dumped from a small paper bag into the bottom of her cup. She knew that valerian root had some of the same properties as valium, and was kind of like a drug, but she had been using it at night, desperate to get some sleep.

Finn sat down at the kitchen table, and a moment later saw her mom's car lights pulling down the driveway. She felt a mixture of annoyance and relief, her primary impulses in parenting. It was a constant drain, and yet a constant distraction. Having raised two babies in the past three years, she had only been able to figure out how to relieve the stress of that with drinking and getting high, but it had also served as an excuse. When she had her moments alone or when Evelyn had the kids, she felt like she deserved a break. Drinking and smoking pot were her rewards.

"Hey, Finnie!" her mom said as she came in with Kairo and Josey.

"Mommy!" Kairo ran to her and jumped up on her lap.

"Hi baby, did you have a good time?" asked Finn, running her fingers through his soft, curly top.

"We jumped and jumped and I'm a really fast dancer!" he said.

"I'm a fast dancer, too!" said Josey. "We did drumming and we did bells!"

"Wow! That's great, guys!" Finn said, as Kairo squirmed off her lap and the two of them ran into his room to play.

"How was your meeting?" asked Evelyn.

"Nice, I stopped and saw Lil after."

"Oh, good! How is she?"

"A little zoned out. She was still sleeping when I got there at 3:00. You know, that's the lifestyle. They play all night and sleep all day."

"Teenagers!" said Evelyn with a lighthearted laugh.

"Yeah, well, Hugh's not exactly a teenager, Mom. He's older than me."

"Yeah, but he's very young emotionally. He's like a teenager, too. Why else would he be interested in a sixteen-year-old? Men take a lot longer to get it together. Maybe Lilli and Hugh will figure it all out at the same time," she said, always the optimist.

"Well, that's very generous of you, Mom," said Finn. "You want some tea? The water's still hot."

"Sure, I'm pretty beat. These kids wear you out!"

"I know, believe me," said Finn, putting the kettle back on for a minute and getting a cup for her mom.

"Wait until you're my age, it's even harder! I don't know what I would have done if I didn't have you, Finn. Raising Josey by myself, trying to work these past few years alone, it would have been impossible."

"Well, it worked out for both of us," said Finn honestly. She stood by the stove.

"It's just so bizarre, you know. Like, what is the universe trying to tell me? Your dad dies before you're even born, then Lilli's father dies when she's three, and Josey's dad when she's still a baby. Why am I supposed to raise daughters with no fathers?"

"Maybe we're meant to be both mothers and fathers to our kids. That's what made it easier when Jake left me. I thought about all the mothers who had raised their kids without dads around. It wasn't like I was the first one to do it. Women have been doing it for centuries."

"You're right about that. Men have been out there, sowing their oats, getting gored by wild boar, killing each other in battlefields. Someone's got to stay home and take care of the little ones," she said.

Finn poured her mom's tea and brought it to the table. "It's lemon, okay?"

"Perfect."

"Mom, what was my father like?" Finn asked, feeling the risk of asking, but since her mom had brought it up first, dared to venture. She thought this might be a safer topic than asking what happened to him or why she couldn't contact his family. It had been on her mind a lot since getting clean, a missing part of her history that she felt might make some kind of sense in the larger scheme of her life.

Evelyn clouded over, but answered, "Oh, honey, he was amazing. He was the most beautiful man, inside and out."

"But you only knew him for a little while, right?"

"Yes, not long enough... he was incredible. I remember when I met him I thought he was the blackest man I had ever seen. So dark, it was startling for me. I'm embarrassed to say this, but it was almost hard for me to look at him."

"Really?"

"Yes. I was kind of a naïve schoolgirl back then, and even though I was fighting for civil rights and had joined the movement here up North, it was more of an abstract thing for me. More about justice, and not about real, actual Black people. When I went down to Alabama, the real, actual Black people there were so different from the ones I knew in the North. I had been hanging out with a bunch of hippies and musicians, some of them black, but it was really a different crowd. The friends I had were interested in equality as a philosophical issue. In the South, it was about survival. What a different world! It was cruel, Finn, you wouldn't believe. Black folks were barely treated like humans."

"Where in Alabama?" asked Finn, digging. She knew she was pushing it.

"Oh, I don't remember," said Evelyn, evasively. "It was during summer break after my first year of college. We went down for a protest, me and three friends from school. I was early admission, so they were a few years older than me. I was only seventeen. My friend Ginny was with her boyfriend, George. I guess I was supposed to be with the other boy, Chuck. I didn't really like him like that, but we all wanted to make a difference and he was nice, so I went along." Finn had heard that part before. "Your dad was part of a church group we met up with there. He was so...polite, soft-spoken, but firm, too. It was the middle of summer, but he always wore a button up shirt and tie. They all did, the black men down there in the movement. They were very clean-cut. It was the only defense they had. I guess they didn't want to give anyone a reason to give them any trouble. It was such a contrast to me and my hippie friends in our rags and fringes. Finnian had the most penetrating eyes, like he could look right into my soul. I was pretty intimidated by him at first." She paused.

Hearing Evelyn speak her father's name, the name that was her own name, was disorienting. "And you fell in love with him?" Finn asked, not wanting her mother to stop the story. This was more than she had ever told her.

"I couldn't help it. He was so smart, so...intense."

Finn waited, but Evelyn didn't continue. "So what happened, Mom? I'm dying to know. I need to know."

Evelyn looked distressed and her eyes filled. "You think you do, Finnie, but you really don't want to know."

"Yes I do, Mom. It's not fair. I know whatever happened hurt you, but I'm not a little kid anymore. I want to know what happened to my father."

"I'm sorry, Finn. I can't really talk about it. I've never talked about it... to anyone. You don't know what you're asking."

Finn sighed. It was so unlike her mom. She was an open book, with her opinions on the tip of her tongue. Her mother would talk to her candidly about anything she asked, sex, drugs, anything.
Except about this one topic. It had always been off-limits. Finn had learned to avoid it, but now, at this point in her life when she was facing all the painful truths about herself, the things she had avoided, she felt like she wanted everything out on the table. "Are you ever going to tell me?" she asked, afraid that the answer might be an absolute 'no.'

"I'm tired, Finn. I need to take Josey home to bed. I know you probably need to know at some point. I know it's been hard on you, too, wondering all these years. I can tell you that your father was a wonderful man, and that he died too young."

"But why... and how?" Now that the subject was finally broached and a little sliver of a window into the past was leveraged, Finn had trouble letting it slam shut, afraid that her mother would lock it away forever and she would never have another opportunity.

"It was bad, Finn. There are really evil people in the world," she gulped and started to quietly sob. Finn had never seen her mother cry like that. She always kept her chin up as a rule.

"I'm sorry, Mom. I'm sorry. It's okay. You can tell me another time... when you're ready."

"I have to be honest, Finn," her mom said between sobs. "I don't know if I'll ever be ready."

♦ ♦ ♦

Her mom had taken Josey home to bed, and Finn was alone with Kairo. She helped him get his pajamas on and brush his teeth, things she never seemed to have the energy for when she was getting high. She read him a book and then lay in bed with him.

"Whattsa madder, Honey?" he asked her. He had gotten into the habit of calling her "Honey" when she was upset, like she said to him when he was upset.

"Oh, nothing, Ro. I'm just thinking."

"What you thinking about?" his husky, sweet little voice moved her and she turned toward him and saw this beautiful, amazing little boy in a way she had never seen him before, not as a child, a needy baby, but as a person. He was a person she had made and who adored her, even with all of her imperfections and mistakes. He was totally unbiased by all of the bad things she had done, all of the wrong and selfish choices she had made. She felt awash with gratitude looking at him, his big brown eyes open wide with complete faith and trust in her.

"Just about how much I love you, and how lucky I am," she said.

"Then why are you sad?" he asked.

"You know what, I'm not really sad, Ro. I have you, and you're the most precious, wonderful boy in the whole world. I'm so lucky that you're my son."

"I'm lucky, I have a mommy like you," said Ro.

After he was asleep, Finn did some hard thinking. With emerging clarity, she realized how everything she had been doing for the past three years was focused on herself and getting her own needs met. She had taken care of Kairo's basic needs, but she was not really present. She loved Kairo deeply, but never really knew how to take care of him other than to keep his diaper clean and keep him fed. She was too preoccupied with going out drinking, obsessing over one relationship or another, trying to get a spare moment to get high. He had been a responsibility, one that she tried to attend to, but in reality she had mostly felt burdened by it. It hadn't helped that she had been raising two babies, then two toddlers. With her compromised stability, doing double the work made it harder to cope with parenting one-on-one in any kind of healthy way. She had been just scraping by, but was not enjoying it at all.

All in a revelatory wash of guilt, Finn realized how unfair this was to Kairo. She had always felt self-righteous because she had stuck around for him. Jake had pursued his tumbleweed lifestyle, backpacking cross-country and eating out of dumpsters while she stayed home, on welfare, but taking care of their son. She suddenly realized that she had been almost as absent in Kairo's life as Jake had been, without even the excuse of being simply not around. She felt this almost like a physical pain in her chest and in her heart. Having nothing to medicate this particular pain, she sat there, just feeling it.

Finn looked at the clock. She could probably call Janie, although she might already be in bed. She was tired of waking her up with this or that emotional drama, though. She was starting to feel like a whiner. She felt like she should be able to figure out how to handle this. She thought about what Janie would probably tell her, to pray. Although Finn had been talking to "God" or "the Universe" as she liked to call it, she had not really embraced the idea that she should pray on her knees, like Janie suggested. It seemed so old fashioned and degrading.

"My God wouldn't want me on my knees," she told Janie.

"Okay, well everybody has a different relationship with their higher power. It's not for me to tell you how to do it, but just do it somehow that makes sense to you. I just know until I started praying on my knees, I don't think God took it seriously, because *I* wasn't really taking it seriously," Janie had said.

Finn didn't know if she was taking it more seriously or not, but with that knife in her chest, she knew she needed help. She got on her knees next to the bed and put her hands together, feeling a little foolish, like a caricature of a little girl in church, here's the steeple.

She said, out loud: "God, I could really use some help here. I know I've really screwed up. I've been a bad mom, a bad girlfriend, generally just a bad person. I want to be better. I don't want to hurt people anymore, and I especially don't want to hurt Kairo. I just don't know how to be a mom to him," she said, and with this admission, tears started flowing. "I don't know what I'm doing, and I really need some help. I want to make it up to him. He deserves it, he really does. He deserves to have a good mom!" she sobbed. The tears broke out of her chest, splintering the pain that had accumulated there and tossing it in every direction.

Finn cried for several more minutes, there on her knees. The crying was a kind of a prayer, and she didn't even feel the need to say anymore. When she was all done and all the tears dissolved, she got up and without brushing her teeth or doing any of her other nighttime stuff, crawled right into Kairo's bed next to him with her clothes on. For the first time since she got sober, Finn fell directly to sleep and slept soundly through the night.

Part III:

November 18-20, 1988

Chapter 9: Pots & Pans

Sadie

Sadie hated being home. She tried to avoid it as much as possible. The little house she shared with her father was dark and filled with unpleasant emotions. She had lived there most of her life, and had some nice childhood memories. Since her mother left when she was 12, though, it held no joyful associations. She entered the kitchen where her father was sitting, slumped over a cup of coffee. She was just coming home from work, and he was getting ready to go to work. He worked the night shift in the treatment plant on the edge of town, and had done so for as long as Sadie could remember.

"Hey, Dad," she said. He stirred from his stupor

and looked up.

"Oh, hi Honey," he said. His face had gotten worn and sunken in the past few years. Having his wife leave and raising two teenagers alone had taken a toll on him. Sadie's brother, Mack, had left to go to technical school a few years earlier, but still came home sometimes on weekends.

"Is Mack coming home this weekend?" Sadie wanted to know. It was Friday, and this information would affect how she planned her weekend, if she tried to stay out or came back home again.

"I don't know, I haven't heard from him," he said. "I think he's on vacation next week for Thanksgiving, though, so I'm sure he'll be home then, at least. I know, I miss him, too. I have the holiday off this year, though, so we'll be able to be together," he said.

"Great," Sadie said, dreading the idea of a heat-and-serve turkey dinner eaten in silence with her father and brother at their cramped kitchen table. Then football and drinking. She'd be sure to miss that, making some excuse about celebrating with friends in town. They lived on the outskirts, and it was only a quick car ride, or if necessary, a long walk away. No matter how inhospitable the social scene became in town, it was still light years better than the repressed climate of her home life.

It had been fine when her mom was around, maybe not idealistic, but pretty wholesome. Mom worked part-time at the diner during the day, home by the time Sadie and Mack got home from school, and dad worked at night. They usually had a rushed dinner together after dad woke up and before he left for work. There wasn't too much overlap, but they did have some family vacations, camping by the shore, or going upstate to stay in a cheap motel for a few days, going to a variety of neglected theme parks. Sadie never had any idea that there was anything unhappy about her parents' marriage, but looking back, she could see that they had designed their worlds to have as little to do with each other as possible.

Regardless of how her parents' relationship appeared in retrospect, it seemed to come out of the blue the morning Sadie and her brother woke up and their mother was gone. Their father came home to find the letter on the table explaining that she had fallen in love with a traveling salesman and was leaving with him. She said that she would be serving their father divorce papers so that she could marry the salesman, but they never came. There was also a brief note to Sadie and Mack, telling them that she loved them very much and that she hoped that they would understand someday why she had to leave. She said she would be in touch with them soon, but they had never heard from her again. Over the years, Sadie had concluded that she must have died. It was the only thing that could explain the total lack of contact. Maybe the salesman was an ax murderer and had killed her as soon as she left and had dumped her body in the swamps at the edge of town. That would explain the absence of even a phone call.

Being twelve and fourteen, Sadie and Mack went on as usual, going to school with their dad sleeping during the day, coming home after school to see if there was any word from Mom. Six months went by, and their dad was drinking a lot more. When he was home he was sitting at the table in the kitchen, not unlike how Sadie had found him that evening, eyes glazed and slumped over a beer. He would also sometimes drink gin and tonic in his bedroom, sitting fully clothed on the bed watching their 12-inch black and white T.V. with the door open. Their dad never really talked about their mom leaving or how it might be affecting them. If they brought it up, like where she might be or why she might not be in touch, he would shrug and say "I don't know, kids. I just don't know."

He was obviously deeply pained and mourning the loss of his wife. The housework piled up, and his hygiene suffered. In one way, this was helpful to Sadie. She was so concerned and sad for her father that it took the focus off of her own grief. After a few months, she made the conscious decision to replace her mother. She came home from school one day and took a look at the kitchen, piled with dirty pots and pans, reeking with overflowing garbage, surfaces splattered with grease and dried food. It was as if they were still waiting for Mom to come home to clean up the mess. She suddenly realized that if she didn't do it, nobody would. It took her most of the afternoon, but by dinnertime when her dad woke up, she had the kitchen cleaned and had made macaroni and cheese, and had even heated up a can of green beans.

"Oh, thanks Honey. You didn't have to do that," her dad said when he walked in. But she knew she did. He sat down, and didn't say another word. From then on, it was just expected that Sadie would cook and clean, and she did, usually without any thanks or acknowledgment. Her father had gotten a prescription for valium to help him sleep when he got home from work, and she didn't know if it was that, or the loss, or the drinking, but he was barely present even when he was home and awake. He stared into space or at his beer, and would only talk if directly asked a question, and then it would usually take him a minute to register and respond in as few words as possible.

Her brother was starting to act out at school, not surprisingly, but with each call from the school or letter in the mail, her father would just shrug and shake his head. "That's what happens when mothers leave their children," he would say. They were left alone a lot, Sadie and Mack, every evening when their dad was at work. When he was not working he was sleeping or drunk. They had always had the normal squabbling and sibling rivalry that comes with kids being spaced only a few years apart, but lately Mack had gotten more intense. He was getting bigger, and would hold Sadie down and tickle her viciously or pinch her or punch her in the arm when she walked by, laughing sadistically. To try to quell his attacks, Sadie worked to try to bond with him, watching the shows he wanted to watch and making him his favorite foods.

When their dad was at work, they would sit on the couch and eat a whole half gallon of ice cream together, and sometimes would dip into his liquor, which was kept on an open shelf in the pantry. He never noticed, or if he did, never said anything. Sadie wanted to prove to Mack how tough she was, so she would always drink whatever concoction he mustered up. One Friday night when their dad was working, Mack mixed up a shake of ice cream and rum. It was awful-tasting and delicious all at once, and Sadie wolfed it down and asked Mack for more. They were laughing, watching *Stripes* on the T.V., and goofing off. Sadie was pleased that he seemed to be enjoying her company, and tried to impress him with her willingness to drink right along with him.

The night got blurrier, and they kept laughing and making more concoctions, and another Rated "R" movie came on. It was dark, with only the light from the T.V. in the living room. Mack started to tickle her and she tried to get up and he tackled her and pinned her down to the floor. She was laughing and shrieking, and trying to crawl away from him, but he kept dragging her back down onto the rug. Sadie was only wearing one of her dad's big t-shirts and her underwear and the shirt kept riding up. She tried to pull it back down to cover her while also trying to ward off Mack's assault. All of a sudden he was clawing at her underwear, pulling them down and off. This was different from their normal rough play. Sadie panicked, not sure what was happening, and started to scream, but Mack held his hand over her mouth. Sadie was scared, flailing out and trying to get away. Mack was so much bigger, and held her down easily, with his shoulder muffling her face. Before she knew what was going on, she felt him prying her legs apart and shoving his penis inside her. There was a sharp pain, and Mack grunted.

He lay there on top of her for a second, then pushed away and got up. "I'm going to bed," he said and left the room. Sadie lay there, dazed and unable to move, with the television still blaring and flashing its incandescent light over the four walls of their sparse living room. After a few minutes, she reached around and found her underwear. She stood up and something oozed out of her. She mopped it up with her underwear, and saw in the eerie light what appeared to be black blood and pearly slime. The next morning, Mack didn't look at her. He walked around the kitchen, slamming cabinets, and acting as if she wasn't even there.

Sometimes Sadie wondered, or maybe wished, that it was just a drunken misunderstanding, and maybe it hadn't really happened the way she remembered it. They were pretty inebriated, after all; maybe she was just confused. Mack and Sadie barely spoke in the following years. The tickling and banter stopped, but so did any kind of communication at all. Because a total absence of interaction was how her father functioned in general, he did not notice any difference between his kids. Sadie was relieved when Mack finally went away to school. Needless to say, she did not look forward to his visits home, and tried to avoid him whenever he was there. He had begun to talk to her again, but always in a detached way, and he still avoided any kind of eye contact.

"You got plans tonight?" her dad asked.

"Uh, no, not really. I was just going to take a shower, go to town, maybe stop by my friend Ella's house," she said.

"Ella... yeah, you've stayed at her house a few times, right?"

"Uh, yeah, that's right." She was surprised he remembered. Not that he ever said anything if she stayed out all night, but she had told him she had stayed at Ella's just in case he cared enough to be concerned at her overnight absences. She was turning nineteen in a few days, so it wasn't like she needed to account for her whereabouts. Even though he did not seem to notice when she was missing, she still felt some pressure to reassure him. As long as she was working, he seemed to feel like she was doing okay and didn't bother himself much with the details. Apparently, he didn't think it was strange that she never brought home any friends and had never had a boyfriend.

Sadie kissed the top of her dad's head. He smiled vaguely and said, "Love you, Sweetie."

"Love you, too, Dad. Have a good night at work." She went off to jump in the shower. She liked to bathe at the end of her shift to get all the griddle grease and burnt coffee smell out of her skin and hair. She dressed, not too particularly, but picked out her nicest underwear, just in case. She had decided to go see Raiche, and was heading to the Trash House. She hadn't heard from him all week, not that he ever asked her for her phone number, but he knew where she worked. She still did not know how to interpret her modeling session with him from the week before. She had decided to risk going there to see where things stood.

She started walking. It was pretty cold, even

with her boots and leather jacket. It would take her a good 45 minutes, walking briskly, to get all the way downtown. After a few minutes, she heard honking and Bram, Raiche's drummer, pulled over in his old Ford Fairlane.

"Hey Sadie, you need a ride?" he asked.

"Sure, thanks!" she jumped into the warm front seat, and thought guiltily that this was the car she had messed around with Hugh in. She wondered if Bram knew or really didn't care as Hugh had told her when they slept together in the back seat that summer.

"Where you going? He asked. Bram was a nice, long-haired hippie who worked in the tie-dye factory. Sadie knew he had a girlfriend of many years and was pretty stable in the scene. In the tightly woven underground of Little Heart, punks and hippies intermingled, and even made their music intersect, playing in bands together. Bram seemed out of sync with the other guys he played with in Preying Menace. He was unusually good-natured and did not get sucked into the womanizing and destruction of his band-mates, but loved to jam and played hard.

"I was heading to the Trash House," Sadie said, uncomfortable with what Bram might think, knowing he probably knew about the poster campaign and had maybe even seen Raiche's recent drawings of her.

"Oh, I live right by there- I'll drop you off. You going to see Raiche?" Bram asked.

"Yeah, I was just going to stop by, but I'm actually heading to Ella's after."

"Ahhh," Bram said, as if this made sense to him. "Yeah, Ella's got some good shit this week. It's got all these little purple and red hairs, like the bud you see in *High Times*! Mind-blowing. You going there to cop or are you friends with her?"

"Um... I guess both. She definitely has great weed. I've been hanging out there a lot, though. I spent the night there a few times when I got stuck in town. She's been really kind to me," she said, and realized this was true.

"Lucky. Anyone who has Ella for a friend doesn't need any other friends!" Bram joked.

"Yeah," said Sadie, smiling. They chatted lightly, and in a minute, pulled down Chapel Street. The Trash House was a big putrid yellow thing, set back on a barren lawn. Individually rented rooms were inhabited by an ever-shifting variety of musicians, punks, and druggies. "Hey, Bram, thanks a lot," said Sadie.

"Sure, no problem," said Bram. "And Sadie..."

"Yeah?"

"Be careful, okay?" his brow was furrowed, and Sadie could see he was not joking.

"Uh, yeah, sure, okay," said Sadie, a little unsettled. "Thanks for the ride." She slammed the door and walked up to the porch, wondering what Bram knew or what he thought about her. She rang the bell, her nerves jostling, not sure what she would even say to Raiche if he was there. A minute went by and nothing, so she rang the bell again. A sleepy metalhead who had a room on the second floor opened the door.

"Hey, Bobby," said Sadie.

"Hey... Sadie, right? What's up?"

"Here to see Raiche."

"Okay," he held the door and she walked in and up the stairs. Raiche's room was right off the second floor landing. She went to go knock, but then noticed that there was a small padlock on the outside of the door, a good indication that he was out. "Oh," she turned around to see Bobby, about to disappear into his room. "Looks like he's not here," she said.

"He'll probably be back soon," said Bobby. "You can wait upstairs if you want." He closed his door without waiting for a response. Sadie paused for a minute, then went down the hall and up the second flight of stairs to the third floor. It was a big open attic room with slanted ceilings and dormers put in to give it more space. It served as a living room and a kitchen, but Sadie had only been in it for shows when Preying Menace played and the floor was slick with sweat and beer. The crusty couches were pushed back and a distinct smell of stale beer, rotting food, and cigarettes permeated the air. The sink and the entire counter, stove, and even the kitchen table was piled with cans, dirty dishes, glasses, pots and pans. Sadie didn't know where to sit, since the couch reeked and looked like it could get up and walk away.

She walked around the perimeter of the room, looking at photos, old band posters, hand-drawn comic strips, and magazine clippings covering the walls. She was relieved that the poster of her butt was not there. After a few minutes, she started to feel very awkward, waiting there, uninvited.

Raiche might or might not show up, and would not even know she was waiting upstairs even if he did get home and went straight to his room. She started to leave, but then stopped at the top of the stairs. She had an idea. Walking over to the kitchen, she moved a few pots and saw a smelly old decrepit sponge. She took it between two fingers, took the least dirty small pan, and put it on the stove with some water. This was no small feat, since to even clear a burner on the stove she had to move several rancid pans and cooking sheets, caked with burned crust of…something… onto the kitchen table.

When the small amount of water boiled she dropped the sponge in, and began clearing out a sink. She found some cleaning supplies and cleaned out one sink and began filling it with soapy water. When the sponge was sterilized, she began to clean for real, systematically moving piles of moldy dishes, scraping food into the trash, and throwing out old cans filled with slime.

She heard steps on the stairs and held her breath, keeping her focus on the sink.

"Oh, hey Sadie. I thought I heard something," it was Kevin, one of Raiche's bass players. "What are you up to?"

"Oh, I was just waiting for Raiche to get home and thought I'd help out," said Sadie, trying to be casual. "I've been to lots of parties here, so… it's the least I could do."

"Oh, that's really cool. Thanks a lot!" said Kevin.

"No problem," said Sadie, continuing her expunging. Kevin got some peanut butter from the fridge and one of the spoons Sadie had just washed and went back downstairs.

Sadie did her best with the little counter and drying space there, and worked her way through most of the dishes, pots and pans, filling the sink again to clean the rest of the silverware and glasses. She was making good progress. There was something very satisfying about making a dent in the disorder. She heard steps on the stairs and this time it was Raiche.

"What's up, Sadie?" he said, not seeming surprised at all to see her cleaning his kitchen.

"Oh, I was just cleaning up a little. I stopped by to see you, and I decided to help out a little. No big deal."

"You came to see me?" said Raiche, a mischievous grin forming on his face.

"Yeah," she said meeting his eyes, then blushing and turning back toward the sink, hiding her embarrassed smile. Raiche went to the fridge and took a jug of milk out and drank right from the container. He stood with the door open watching her, and took another swig.

"Well, when you're done, why don't you stop down to see me?" he said. He put the milk back, closed the door, and trotted down the stairs.

Sadie hesitated, not sure if he meant she should finish cleaning the kitchen, or come down now. She was almost done anyway, so she washed a few more items, did the best she could to finish patching up the wreckage, drained the sink, and after drying her pruney hands on a suspicious-looking towel, headed downstairs.

Chapter 10: Full House

Ella

Ella was not in the mood for a party. She had promised Cooper that Carbon could play at her apartment that night, but honestly did not have any desire to have her house trashed and her eardrums shattered. It was good for business, though. She had calculated that she needed to move 20 more bags that weekend to meet her own self-imposed quota and could probably sell a dozen that night. She had not been smoking herself. It had started to make her twitchy. Weed had always been her friend, but lately it just seemed to make her crispy and tired. She was very good at modulating her own environment, so she drank more tea and water and tried to flush out her crankiness and irritability.

Ella attributed her moodiness to her total detox.

She had not only given up weed, but she had also not had sex in over a week. After alienating the kid, Darien, and pushing away the pusher, Seth, there was no one left. Ella could have easily walked down to Market Street and found a new sex partner in less than five minutes, and had been known to do that when struck with a particular brand of boredom, but she was grieving. She missed the tower. She missed seeing it outside her window and mostly, she missed living in the attic. She yearned for the dark and dusty floorboards and the smell of pigeon shit. She yearned to be the Tower Ella.

This girl with long legs and long hair who laughed and flirted and held beer parties, that was not the Tower Ella. The Tower Ella read voraciously, studying the complexities of human cultures, absorbing literature for hours in the wan daylight filtered through the round attic windows. The Tower Ella heated water on a little hotplate to pour over herbs for her tea while sewing her own bedding and making hand-stitched fabric pouches to sell weed in, her first marketing invention. She was completely and authentically on her own there. Now, regularly surrounded by people, it disguised the reality that she was still completely on her own.

She had always reserved the idea that she could go back and live in the tower if she ever wanted. Now, every time she walked by her kitchen window, she saw the gap in the sky where the tower used to be as a knife to her heart. She stared at it now as she sipped her tea, that piece of sky which represented the end of her safe haven, the end of Tower Ella. Kelpie made a little whining sound and Ella looked down at her. No Kelpie in the tower, the only thing bad about it. She patted her friend on the head and scratched behind her chocolate ears. There was a brief knock on the door, and Coop stumbled in lugging a guitar amp. He put the amp down and stood up, rubbing his back.

"Are you ready for a revolutionary night of groundbreaking music, Ella?" he asked, leaning over to attack Kelpie with killer bats. Kelpie circled him, playfully air-biting.

"Of course," Ella lied.

"Good, because we are going to break the sound barrier. All life will cease to exist and the earth will reverse on its axis. Just wait, it's going to be monumental."

"Okay. I'm ready," said Ella, chuckling. Cooper's grandiosity was one of the things she found endearing about him.

"Sandler is getting the keg," he informed her. Great. She hated seeing Sandler. He was another one who had gotten clingy after she played sheet hockey with him, and now gave her moony sad puppy eyes whenever she encountered him. Nothing could be more boring.

"Hey Coop, listen, I'm going to go lie down for a few minutes. Will you get everybody set up?"

"Okay. You okay, Ella?" asked Cooper with uncharacteristic concern. Cooper was so self-absorbed that he usually did not notice anyone else.

"Yeah, just tired. Didn't sleep well last night. It's

so friggin' hot in here." That was true. The heat was broken on full blast and she had to keep the windows open to let in the cold November air.

Ella took Kelpie and went to her bedroom. She curled up in her cave with her dog and quickly passed out. She didn't know how long she slept, but she awoke to guitars tuning up, shuffling and stomping around, and multiple loud conversations in the living room. She opened her door and found about a dozen people milling around, smoking and running cables. A kid she didn't know was setting up his drum kit against the back wall, and a few more people in the kitchen were hovering around the keg.

"Hey Ella, where are the cups?" Cooper shouted to her.

"Nobody brought cups?" Ella asked, annoyed.

Sandler was standing there, his floppy hair hanging over to one side and his hands shoved into his jean pockets, looking sheepish. "Yeah, Cooper told me to pick up the keg, but I didn't think to get the cups. I'll go back out and get them. Want to take a ride with me, Ella?"

"No, I better stay here. People will be showing up soon," she said.

Sandler's face dropped. "Okay, I'll be back in a few."

"Great, thanks," said Ella, not meeting his eyes. The sad puppy face had not worked yet, but it did not keep him from trying. He stood there for a minute, as if she might change her mind, then sighed and turned toward the door, making long strides with his beat up jump boots. He was really cute, and could be a lot of fun when he wasn't sulky. Men are big fucking babies, she told herself. She began setting up the kitchen, pushing the table and chairs against the wall, making room for the crowd of people that would undoubtedly begin showing up.

Jack and Ditto came in. "Leave the door open," Ella told them. It was getting stuffy already and moving the chairs was making her even hotter. "Okay you guys, you ready to work?"

They bobbed their heads and grinned. "We're your men, Ella."

"Well, I don't know about that, but you can definitely collect money at the door," Ella joked and they laughed at her dis. "You guys do a good job like last time and I'll toss you a dime to share."

"What, no advance?" they asked, holding out their hands. "How's a guy supposed to work with no weed? That's just inhumane."

"Okay, okay, don't call the labor police," she fetched a tiny bag and handed it to Jack who greedily opened it and sniffed it. Ditto took it and did the same.

"You got a pipe?" asked Jack.

"Amateurs!" said Ella, shaking her head. She opened a kitchen drawer and took out a little glass pipe, handed it to them, and walked away to see how the band was setting up in the living room. Cooper was directing traffic and loudly bellowing about the grandeur of the evening while slugging a forty.

"Couldn't wait for the keg, Coop?"

"Never enough, Ella, never enough! Had to prime the pump. It's a big night, Carbon's introduction to Little Heart. Things will never be the same. Hey, it was Sandler's birthday yesterday. We should sing him a birthday ballad. I gotta talk to Raiche, we'll do a Carbon version of *Happy Birthday*.

"Sounds like a great idea."

"Where is Raiche anyway? He should be here already."

"Haven't seen him yet."

Ditto yelled from the kitchen, "He's with Sadie *Lain*. Probably getting *Lain!*" he cracked himself up and he and Jack cackled and convulsed with the joke, smacking each other on the backs and congratulating each other for their cleverness.

"You guys are brilliant," said Ella.

At that moment, Raiche came in the door with his guitar and Sadie followed behind. This set Jack and Ditto into a new set of squealing laughter.

"Three bucks, Sadie Lain," they said shoving their hands in Sadie's face. Sadie brushed their hands away.

"Two bucks!" yelled Cooper from the living room. "We advertised two bucks, it's the Carbon special. Once everyone knows us they'll pay more. Plus, it's a birthday party- it's Sandler's birthday. It's the birthday keg party discount."

"Okay, Cranky," said Jack.

"Oh shit," said Raiche. "I forgot it was Sandler's birthday yesterday!"

"Yeah, we gotta totally bastardize *Happy Birthday* for him," said Cooper. "We'll rip it to shreds, make it beg for mercy. What do you think? Can we put it in? Let's practice!" Raiche started setting up his guitar and the two started to mutilate chords vaguely resembling the birthday song.

"Wow," said Ella to Sadie. "That is going to be pretty...interesting." They laughed. A few minutes later, Sandler returned with the cups and found the keg party had turned into a birthday party for him. They tapped the keg and people started to arrive for the show. It took a while for Cooper to locate his bass player, who had gotten lost trying to find the right apartment, but eventually the music began.

Ella lasted about five minutes, then headed toward her room. Sadie was standing by the front, watching Raiche. Ella tugged on her sleeve and gesturing, pulled her into the bedroom. She shut the door and the shrieking guitar duos became slightly less ascorbic. Sadie looked confused about why Ella had dragged her in there. "I can't stand the noise. I love Coop, but that shit is just insane. As if one rancid guitar is not enough!"

"Oh," said Sadie. "I actually really like Raiche's playing."

"Hey, if you want to watch the show, go ahead, I just thought I'd rescue you from having your brain melt."

"No, no, no, I'm fine. I'd actually rather be in here," admitted Sadie. She paused. "I'm not sure what I'm doing here anyway."

"Well, it looks like you're with Raiche, aren't you?"

"I guess so, I mean, I carried his bag here."

"So he asked you to come with him?"

"Well, sort of. I was down at the Trash House, then he had to come here, so I just kind of came with him, but I don't know if I'm really *with* him."

"But you were at his house?"

"Well, yeah, but I wasn't really even invited there. I just kind of showed up. I wanted to talk to him about last weekend. About the... modeling session."

"Oh," said Ella. "Was this the first time you saw him since the 'modeling session'?" Sadie nodded. "So what did he say?"

"Nothing really," she said. "He showed me a few of the drawings he'd been working on and said he wanted to draw me again sometime."

"I'll bet he does."

"Yeah, so then he needed to come here, so we just packed up and came over. We didn't really end up talking about anything."

"That's so surprising because Raiche is usually such a great communicator."

"Yeah, well, it's my own fault. I didn't really bring it up and I didn't ask him what's going on between us. I didn't really have time, but I probably wouldn't have anyway."

"Sadie, why are you always blaming yourself for other people's shit?"

"What do you mean?"

"Well, I have so many examples I can't even choose just one, but now you're even blaming yourself for Raiche's lack of communication!"

"Yeah, but this isn't just something that happened to me. I got myself into it."

"Not by yourself. You sleep with him, he trashes you, you model for him, he acts like nothing happened," she said, getting agitated.

"Yeah, and then I go and do his dishes," Sadie mumbled to herself.

"You what?"

"I did his dishes. I mean, the dishes at the Trash House. I washed them, cleaned the whole kitchen really, while I was waiting for him to get home."

"Um... I'm speechless."

"Really? Well, that's rare."

"You cleaned his fucking kitchen?"

"Well, it's a lot of people's kitchen. It was really trashed. Ha! It really is a Trash House."

"I just don't even know what to say."

"Well, I was waiting for him, I was bored, and I didn't want to just sit around, so I cleaned. It was really dirty. Somebody needed to clean it."

"I think that might be the most pathetic thing I've ever heard," said Ella, shaking her head.

"Maybe you could go back to being speechless."

"Sadie, do you have any idea what a fool you're being?"

"Well, maybe I am, maybe I'm not. I don't know yet."

"You don't? You mean, you still have some hope that he really likes you? That he wants to be your boyfriend?"

"Maybe. I don't know. I know I really like him."

"Well, here's a newsflash, Sadie: HE DOESN'T LIKE YOU! You're a fool that he fucked, humiliated, and now is following him around like an abused dog, looking for a scrap or a pat on the head."

"That's really shitty, Ella. You're not a nice person."

"Why? Because I'd rather you hear the truth from me than spend the next month getting shit on only to find that exactly what I just said is true? Believe it or not, Sadie, I actually like you. This is me liking you!"

"I'd hate to see you not liking me."

"If I didn't like you I wouldn't say anything. I'd sit there and watch you squirm and chase him around, like the rest of the town is doing. I would be a bystander to one of the most classic cases of... Raiche-ism that has ever happened in Little Heart."

"Raiche-ism, that's funny, Ella."

"Yeah, it is. I just made that up."

"Well, it's funny."

"I know." They sat looking at each other, then cracked up. There was a knock at the door. "Come in!" yelled Ella.

Hugh came in, followed by Lilli. The raucous noise came in with them. "Hey, Ella! Hi, Sadie." They closed the door behind them and the din subsided a bit.

"Hi guys. It's pretty insane out there, huh?" asked Ella.

"Classic Cooper," said Hugh. "That guy is crazy on the guitar!"

"What are you guys up to? You want to buy a bag?"

"Yeah, I got a job!" said Hugh. "I'm going to be a cook, working nights at *Wing King*. I'm on the 8 P.M. to 4 A.M. shift."

"Cool! So you want to splurge for an eighth, or just a dime?"

"An eighth. Can you front me, though? I don't start until this Wednesday and I don't get paid until Sunday. Is that okay?"

"Sure, anything for an old pal!" said Ella. Lilli looked around the room and shifted from one foot to the other. "What's up Lilli?" asked Ella while she retrieved the bag.

"Not much," said Lilli, forcing a mediocre smile.

"Hey, you got a rolling paper?" asked Hugh. Ella took out some papers and handed them to Hugh with a tray. He sat on the fancy green couch and began rolling, chattering on about his new job. It was still loud, and Ella couldn't really hear everything he was saying, but something about being a manager and in charge of the overnight shift, blah, blah, blah. Lilli sat on the floor with Sadie and Ella, looking up at Hugh. Ella couldn't tell if she was watching him or anticipating the weed, but there was something in her gaze reminiscent of Kelpie when she was waiting for her food. Hugh lit the joint and passed it to Ella.

"I'm fasting," she explained and passed it on to Sadie without taking a hit. Sadie partook and so did Lilli, and then it went back to Hugh and around again, skipping Ella. When it was spent, Hugh stood up and announced he was going back to watch the band. Lilli started to rise, but Ella stopped her: "You can stay in here with us, Lilli." Lilli looked surprised, and looked at Hugh.

"Yeah, why don't you hang out in here with Ella?" said Hugh.

"Okay," said Lilli and stayed put.

"Yeah, stay in with us, we'll have a *yin* party in here," said Ella. "So, Lilli," she said after Hugh had left, "what's the deal? How's life?"

"Pretty good," said Lilli.

"So, listen, I was wondering if you could tell our friend Sadie a little bit about Raiche Cameron. I know you have experience in that department," said Ella. Lilli looked startled and Sadie rolled her eyes, embarrassed. "I mean, what's the real deal with Raiche? Can you fill us in, because Sadie seems to think he might be her Prince Charming."

"Are you with Raiche?" Lilli asked Sadie, with a touch of jealousy.

"No, I mean, not really. I mean... I've been with Raiche, but... I don't really know if we're together."

"Oh," said Lilli. "Yeah, that sounds familiar."

"So you've been through this, too?" asked Ella. "Didn't you used to hook up with him?"

"Yeah, over the summer for a little while. I don't know if we were ever really together, either. He was pretty vague about it, and I thought we were, but then I found out he didn't really take it that seriously."

"Really?" said Ella, with mock incredulity. "So, how did you find out he wasn't really into you?"

"Hugh told me. It's kind of how we got together, actually. Hugh was looking out for me, told me what Raiche was saying about me, that he was using me," said Lilli. She tried to mask her pained expression, but it leaked through. "So, you really like him, Sadie?"

"Yeah, I guess so," said Sadie. "I'm not really sure, I'm just trying to figure out what's going on between us, if there even is an 'us.'"

"Weren't you pissed about the posters, though? You didn't know he was going to do that, did you?" asked Lilli.

"No! Of course not. I think it was supposed to be a joke," said Sadie. Lilli's expression betrayed that she did not seem to be buying that. Sadie continued: "I mean, I didn't know he was going to do it, but it's not really a big deal. I think it's kind of funny now, actually."

Lilli and Ella exchanged glances. Ella said, "Okay, Lilli, now you've known Raiche a long time, even in the biblical sense, so tell me your opinion. What are the chances that Raiche is really into Sadie and wants to be her boyfriend, and is not just playing around with her?"

"Slim to none... Sorry, Sadie."

Sadie looked really uncomfortable. "I don't know. I still need to talk to him," she said.

"Then go talk to him," Ella said. The band had stopped. It sounded like they were taking a break. "Go ahead, we'll wait," said Ella. Sadie hesitated, then stood up slowly. "Go on, what are you waiting for? Don't you want to know?" Sadie gave Ella a deadly look and walked out, closing the door behind her. "This is not going to end well," Ella said to Lilli.

"Yeah, I know," said Lilli. "But do you think maybe he really does like her? I mean, who the hell knows what Raiche likes?"

"C'mon, Lilli, I like Sadie, but she's got 'use me' written all over her."

"Yeah, that's true. I guess I did, too, so he did."

"Yeah, that's advertising that someone like him can't resist. What a sad boy," Ella said, shaking her head.

"Him?"

"Yes. Very sad. Only a very sad boy whose mother didn't love him enough would do that to women."

"Really, you think so?"

"Of course. Why else would he enjoy hurting women so much?"

"I guess I never thought about it like that. It's just what he does. He's pretty cold."

"Or maybe really sad," said Ella.

"It's kind of hard to feel bad for him," said Lilli. "He always seems to come out of everything okay. I mean, look what he did to me. I'm sure you know about the whole thing when they handcuffed me, you know..."

"Everyone knows."

"Yeah, well, then I go and hook up with him after that, so..."

"Yeah, his guilt was absolved."

"Right, because if he really was such a sinister fuck, then why would I go out with him after all that?"

"Yeah, why would you?"

"Right."

"No, I mean, why would you? Really, Lilli. Why

would you?"

"Oh," Lilli shifted. "I guess I didn't like myself that much. I felt like it was my fault. I wanted him to like me, that's why I even went there and put myself in that position anyway. I really liked him. Do you know, Ella, I was so fucked up that night I thought that it was Raiche that I had sex with until days later when I went back to talk to him about it? Then he told me that I had sex with... Kevin Gordon! I didn't even know Kevin, but what the hell did I know, I was practically passed out on my stomach with my hands cuffed behind my back. I felt like such a fuck up and a slut. When Raiche started to seem like he actually liked me... months later... I was grateful."

Ella nodded. "It's so bizarre."

"What do you mean?"

"That Raiche has so much power over so many people. Why would you, why would Sadie, ever make yourselves vulnerable to someone like him? I mean, I think he's hot, too, but I would never in a million years mess with that. He's like a really dangerous horse. Might be pretty to look at, but if you ride him, he'll probably hurt you."

Lilli giggled at the corny analogy, "Yeah, but girls like me and Sadie, we go back for more."

"Exactly. It's like you want to get hurt. Maybe you think you deserve it."

"Yeah, we probably do."

There was a quick knock on the door and it opened. Sadie came in all flushed. She closed the door and stood with her back against it.

"So?" Ella asked. Sadie shook her head and bit

her lip. "What happened?" Sadie sighed and pushed away from the door. She slipped down onto the floor next to Ella and Lilli.

"It's like you said. He's not into me. I'm a fool."

"What happened?" asked Lilli gently.

Sadie took a wavering breath. "He said that he and Kristi got back together. Actually, they've been back together since right after we first hooked up. That's why he didn't sleep with me last weekend, he said." She turned to Lilli to explain, "He drew me naked last weekend, but we didn't have sex. He says it's because now he's back with Kristi, so he still really wants to 'do' me and everything, but doesn't want to cheat on her."

"That asshole," said Lilli. "I'm sorry, Sadie."

"Yeah, well. I should have known."

"Yeah," said Ella. "Well at least now you know. Now you can protect yourself."

"Yeah, but I should have known already. This always happens to me. I wish I was more guarded. I put myself out there and then I get rejected. I just hoped it was different this time."

"This has happened to you before, with other guys?" Lilli asked.

"Yeah, a bunch of times. I mean, I haven't slept with a whole lot of people, but it's happened with every guy I've slept with. I'll like somebody, then I'll sleep with them, and then they avoid me like the plague. I'm almost nineteen and I've never even had a boyfriend. I guess I'm good enough to fuck, but not good enough to be somebody's girlfriend. I don't know why I thought this would be any different."

"Yeah, that used to happen to me all the time, too," Lilli confessed. "Before Hugh. And I did sleep with a lot of people. They all ran the other direction afterward. Then I hooked up with Hugh, and it was finally different, so maybe you just haven't met the right guy yet. And it all started in the back of Bram's car!"

"What did?" asked Sadie.

"Me and Hugh. The first time we hooked up it was in the back of Bram Hanlon's car! We've been together ever since."

"Wow, that's..." Sadie didn't know what to say.

"Yes, Sadie, so if you're really lucky, you can hook up with someone like Hugh, so you just got to go back out there and keep trying," said Ella. Knowing Ella better than she used to, Sadie could see the pointed sarcasm in Ella's suggestion.

"Yeah, I think I'll just keep my pants on for a while."

"Not a bad idea, I might try that myself," said Ella.

Sadie laughed, "Well, we all know that's not likely."

The music started up again, a distorted version of *Happy Birthday*. "That's for Sandler. His birthday was yesterday," explained Ella. "We should go out there." They got up.

"For a second, I thought it was for me," said Sadie.

"Oh yeah, when's your birthday?" asked Lilli as they headed toward the door and the noise.

"It's on Monday. November 21st. I was born on the cusp of Sadge."

"What?" said Lilli.

"The cusp of Sagittarius. I'm a Scorpio, but I'm right on the cusp."

"Oh," said Lilli. "For a second, I thought you said you were born on the cusp of *Sad*."

"Yeah, well, that too."

♦ ♦ ♦

Ella was alone, finally. Well, sort of. Sadie was asleep on her couch, but Ella had gotten used to her, the way she was used to Kelpie being there. She was a companion, but not really an interfering presence. Ella liked having Sadie around. She was kind of a sad sack, tragic figure to Ella, and she felt sorry for her, but there was something really endearing about her, too. She had never really had a close female friend except for Aurora. Even on the island, sometimes children would come and stay there for a while when their mothers were in training, or birthing, and there were always babies, but as a girl she had not really had a true friend except for the animals. They had goats on the island, and Ella spent a lot of time with them, learned to milk them when she could walk. They were good company, with their musky smells and prickly warm udders. But she had never had a human friend until Aurora.

When she met Aurora, she really never needed another friend. They were so tight, right from the beginning, that neither of them really had much need to seek elsewhere. *They* had friends, but neither of them really had separate friendships with individual people. Aurora was her *soulsister,* a piece of herself, like a mirror image even though they looked nothing alike. They understood each other completely. Now, Ella needed to talk to Aurora. It was late in New York, maybe 1 or 2, but it would still be early in Oregon. She untangled her beige phone, plugged its long cord into the wall, and took it down the hall to the bathroom so she wouldn't disturb Sadie.

"Hey, Sis," she heard Aurora's light accented greeting.

"Hi, Rory."

"What's the matter?"

"I have a little problem," said Ella.

"You're pregnant, aren't you?"

"Yes. How did you know?"

"I had a dream last night. You had puppies and you were nursing them."

"Oh, shit, Aurora. I'm really fucked."

"How did this happen? You're so careful."

"I know. But I forgot. There was this guy, he kind of sideswiped me and I got a little disoriented. I forgot to take my wild carrot seed for a few days. Then we fucked. It had to be then. I was careful after that and then I even started using condoms."

"Who's the guy?"

"Some farmer from Iowa. I met him on my trip back from seeing you."

"That was a while ago. Are you that far along?"

"Well, no, I mean, he came to see me here in Little Heart in September."

"So, what are you going to do?"

"What do you mean, what am I going to do?

I'm going to get rid of it, of course. I have the herbs already. It's easy."

"Okay. That's what you want."

"Of course! What the hell else would I do? I can't have a baby!"

"No, of course not."

"But?"

"But, you're calling me, so you must not be sure. Otherwise you would have just done it already."

"Of course I'm sure. There is no alternative."

"What about the guy. Is he still around? Would he want to know about this?"

"Yeah, well, that's actually a funny story. But no, he's not around."

"So...?"

"So, I'm going to go do it now. I just wanted to check in. You know, just in case."

"Well, be careful."

"I will."

"Let me know."

"I will."

"Te amo, Ella."

"Ditto."

Ella hung up and put the phone away and boiled some water. She poured herbs out of little paper bags into her brown teapot: Black & Blue, Copper & Tan, like her mother had taught her. She made it as strong as possible, and while it was steeping, drew a hot bath. She poured a large cup of the dark liquid and put it on the edge of the tub. She lit a few candles, turned out the light, and got in.

The pungent smell of the tea permeated the

air, poisonous and powerful. She had made this remedy for other women in trouble, but had never had to use it herself. She had been careful. The water went up to her chin and her hair floated around her. She looked over the seascape of her breasts, like twin islands, to her small belly submerged under the expanse of water. She stayed, lying still in the tub, until both the water and the tea in the cup had grown cold.

Chapter 11: Injuries

Lilli

Lilli slept in again. She was beat up, although she had taken it light since the mushroom incident. Hugh was still sleeping. He had been up later than she had, staying at the party long into the night. After a trip to the bathroom, Lilli passed by her kitchen window and noticed Sadie and Ella sitting in Ella's living room across the way. She laced up her boots and threw on her jacket, stuffing something into her pocket before going out the door. She knocked on the back door to Ella's apartment a minute later and Kelpie and Ella let her in. Kelpie sniffed her, tickling her legs through her thick black tights.

"Howdy, Lilli! What's up? You don't need another bag already?" Ella asked.

"No, no, actually I came to bring something to

Sadie. Sorry, I saw you two in here from across the street.

"Hi, Lilli," Sadie said, wondering what in the world she could have for her.

"Here." Sadie held out her hand and Lilli dropped something small and round into it. Sadie turned it over and found a little black button with a green "equal" sign on it.

"What is this?"

"Raiche gave it to me, a while ago."

"Um... thanks?"

"I wanted you to have it, for protection." Lilli said, shifting from one foot to the other. "He gave it to me, and it was a total sham. I never understood why he gave it to me, and then last night I realized that he was trying to disarm me. He wanted me to think of myself as an equal partner in what we were doing... but we weren't equal. We were never equal."

"Wow," exclaimed Ella. She was actually impressed. She didn't realize that Lilli was such a deep thinker. Sadie was still really confused. "It's like a warrior amulet," said Ella. "You take a piece of your enemy and it protects you from them," she explained to Sadie.

"Something like that," said Lilli. "I just know how you feel right now, Sadie. This is to remind you what kind of person Raiche really is. He wants you to believe that you're an active participant, but we all know he's the only one calling the shots."

Sadie felt strange getting this gift from Lilli, but touched, too. Nobody ever really gave anything to her, or even gave her much thought. "Thanks,

Lilli. Really, thanks. I'll wear it, and I'll remember."

Lilli nodded promptly, and turned in an almost business-like fashion to leave. "Wait, Lil," said Ella. "Why don't you hang out for a while? Sadie and I were just having tea. You didn't get to finish yours last weekend, so why don't you stay now and have some with us?"

"Oh yeah, sure," said Lilli. "Yeah, last weekend sucked. I was kind of glazed."

"Yeah, you were. You seem better now," said Ella.

"Yeah," Lilli agreed. "Fucking hash... and then mushrooms. Not a good combination."

"I told you, don't fuck around with that hash. And shrooms, too? You can't take those unless you're really spiritually prepared," Ella insisted, pouring Lilli a cup of tea.

"Yeah, well I wasn't," said Lilli.

"No kidding," said Ella. Sadie was still looking at the button, running her fingers over its surface.

"Thank god I was with Hugh, he calmed me down."

"Yeah, thank god for ol' Hugh. He was kind of sloppy last night, huh?"

Lilli looked puzzled, "Not when I left, I went home around midnight. He still seemed okay."

"Oh," said Ella. Sadie seemed to snap to attention. "Yeah, he came back around two. He was kind of wasted."

"He came back, you mean he wasn't here the whole time?"

"No, he left with... a couple of people a little earlier, then came back looking for Raiche."

"Who did he leave with?"

"Um... not sure, that girl, Jenna, and... maybe there were some more people, I think they just went to the bar for a bit."

Lilli felt as if her heart literally flipped over in her chest. Ella and Sadie were saying something else, but she couldn't really pay attention with the blood rushing in her ears. "Sorry, guys. I gotta go home," she started to rise.

"Finish your tea!" Ella commanded. Her tone surprised Lilli, who sat back down. She picked up her cup and obeyed.

"He told me he was at your house," Lilli said weakly.

"He was. He came back."

"Yeah, but he didn't mention going to the bar... with Jenna."

"I'm sure there's an explanation. You can ask him later," Ella's words calmed Lilli down enough to sit and drink her tea. Of course there was an explanation. This was Hugh they were talking about.

"Hey, Lilli, isn't that your sister?" Sadie was looking out the window onto Market Street. Lilli came over and saw Finn, about to go in the door leading upstairs to her apartment. She banged on the window, which was already cracked open due to the stifling heat in the apartment. She opened it further and called to Finnian, who turned and, seeing Lilli, waved and crossed the street, going around to the back of the building.

Ella let her in. Finn gave her a hug and said, "I can't believe how grown up you got!" moving on past her down the hall to hug her sister. "It's been a long time since I was in this apartment."

"You used to hang out here?" asked Ella.

"I used to live here, for almost four years," said Finn. "I moved back to my mom's when I got pregnant with Kairo."

"Woah!" said Ella, "I didn't know that! That's so weird."

"Can I look around? Do you mind?"

"Sure."

Finn poked around in the kitchen and opened the door to the pantry. "Jake lived here."

"With you?" asked Ella.

"No, I mean in this closet. I rented it to him. He put a bedroll down on the floor in here with all his stuff up on the shelves. That's actually how we got together, we were housemates before we were a couple."

Ella, Lilli, and Sadie looked in to the narrow broom closet, trying to imagine someone sleeping in there. Finn walked back to the bedroom and looked around. "Futon in the closet, nice," she commented. "What a beautiful couch! I love the color," she said, noticing the curved loveseat nestled against the wall. There was a copy of Even Cowgirls Get the Blues lying on it. "I love Tom Robbins, she said, "That's one of my favorite books."

"Me too," said Ella, "but Jitterbug Perfume is my all-time favorite." They all went back out to the living room and Ella fetched a cup of tea for Finn.

"I sold a lot of weed in this apartment," reminisced Finn. The other three exchanged glances.

"Really?" said Ella. "That is so interesting. So you were a dealer?"

"The biggest in Little Heart at the time."

"Wow, but you don't do that now, I'm guessing," said Ella.

"No, no, no. I'm sober. I've been clean for over six months now, but I stopped selling a few years back. It was just too risky with the baby."

"Sure," said Ella. "So what made you get sober?"

Finn sighed. Internally, Lilli sighed too, dreading a long speech by her sister. "It just wasn't working for me anymore. I guess I always drank and got high to avoid my feelings, but it was just making it worse. I was constantly humiliating myself and I felt worse and worse all the time."

Sadie was nodding despite herself. "So, what, do you go to meetings or something?"

"Yeah, something like that."

"And it helps?"

"Well, I have to live life on life's terms, but yeah, the meetings help. And I have a good sponsor."

"That's really great, Finn," said Ella. "It's really good to see you, you know our families go back so many years. I remember coming over to your house when I first got to Little Heart. Your mom was always really nice to my mom, and you were always so nice to me."

"Well, we were born in the same place, you know?"

"We were? You were born on the island?"

"Yeah, actually, I think my mom was the one who told your mom about the Colony, when she was pregnant with you. My mom hooked her up with the people down there and then she just didn't come back until... you know, until Catherine died."

"Wow, this is so strange, I never knew that your mom was the one who linked us with the Colony," said Ella.

"I never knew that either," said Lilli. "Okay, well that is just... I had no idea."

"Yeah, Mom went there when she was pregnant with me. She didn't stay long afterward, not like your mom, Ella."

"How did I not know this?" Lilli shook her head.

"Well, I'm lucky I even know that. You know Mom's always been really secretive about my dad, me being born, where I came from."

"Really?" said Finn. "I wonder why?"

"Something happened, I know my dad was killed. She's never told me the details. She doesn't want to talk about it."

"Well she has to," said Ella. "You need to know that. I needed to know about my creepy father even though he wanted nothing to do with me. You need to know your history. It's important."

"Yeah, well tell that to my mom. She won't budge."

"That's just not good enough," said Ella. "Who knows, it might make the whole rest of your life make sense, like with my dad, I know that a lot of my issues with men come from having that jerk reject me and my mom."

"You have issues with men, Ella?" Sadie said deadpan.

"Haha. No, seriously, Finn. It's really important."

"I guess you're right, I'm just not sure how to

convince her."

"You just need to corner her. Find a time when no one else is around and demand that she tell you. It might be painful for her, but you need to know."

"The kids are always around."

"Bring them over to me, Finn," said Lilli. "I'll watch them so you and Mom can talk... I'll do a better job than last time."

"Okay, maybe tomorrow. Hey speaking of the kids, I better get home. Nice to see you, Ella. I'm glad you're taking such good care of my apartment. Bye...Sadie, right?"

She started to leave, then stopped in her tracks looking out the kitchen window. "Oh. Oh yeah, I forgot about the Tower." Ella's attention piqued. "I loved being able to see it from here. You know, I used to get high up there? When I went to school there, eighth grade, we used to sneak up and smoke in the Tower. It's so sad to see it gone."

"Really," said Ella.

Finn departed and Sadie asked Lilli, "Doesn't your sister only have one kid? She said 'kids,'"

"She's talking about our little sister, Josephine, too. Josey's Kairo's age. They're always together.

"Oh. That must be strange, having a little sister the same age as your kid?"

"I've always thought so," said Lilli.

♦ ♦ ♦

Hugh and Lilli were walking along the road to Raymond's house. She had confronted him when he woke up about going to the bar. He reassured her that he just missed going out, that he had really given up going to the bars since they were together because Lilli could not get in to the ones in Little Heart. Jenna was a bartender at Smoochies, so she was able to get him in without a cover charge. She got him a few drinks for free. That was all. Lilli was reassured.

Lilli was filling Hugh in on the visit from Finn at Ella's house.

"It was just so strange, having her there, talking about selling pot in that apartment. She of course had no idea that's exactly what Ella does. And I can't believe she was born on the same island where Ella was born. My mother never told me anything about that! I knew she knew Ella's mother going way back, but I didn't realized that's how she and Ella ended up on the island. Isn't that crazy, Hugh... Hughey?"

Hugh spun around sharply. "Stop calling me Hughey, Lilli! My name's Hugh, not 'Hughey'. You really need to cut that out!"

Lilli just stared at him. He turned around and kept walking. She stood for a few moments, then walked slowly behind him. He walked ahead and didn't even turn around. They got to Raymond's house and went into his bedroom. Raymond and Hugh chatted and started playing around on their instruments. Hugh now kept his bass at Raymond's since they played there so much. Lilli, feeling invisible, sat on the futon, tracing the pattern on the red blanket with her fingertips.

After a few minutes, she took Jitterbug Perfume

out of her bag. She had borrowed it from Ella after hearing it was her favorite. Reading about New Orleans, immortal lovers, trickster horned gods, and olfactory science took her away from her pain temporarily, but she lacked the safety net of the connection with Hugh that had protected her over the last several months. Something had changed and she felt it. Reading about this ancient couple riding out centuries in love together amplified the distance she felt between them.

It was dark when they left. Now that they were alone, Lilli could not let it go, "Did anything happen with Jenna?"

"No, Lilli. Nothing happened. I didn't sleep with her."

"Did anything happen?"

"We took a walk, went up to the playground."

"So nothing happened?"

"Okay, we kissed. That was it."

Lilli felt like a trap door opened up below her heart and her whole world went falling in. She didn't even know how to respond. "I thought... I thought you loved me."

"I do. I do, Lil. It was just a kiss. Look, you don't own me, you know."

"I can't believe you kissed someone else! I thought you were... committed."

"I was, I am. I just need my freedom, too."

"What does that mean?"

"It means I don't know if I can be faithful to you. I mean, I've changed a lot for you. It's a sacrifice. I'm used to going out, doing my own thing. I haven't even been able to go out since we've been together."

"I didn't realize that was so important."

"Well it is. I've been on my own a long time. I'm used to just going to the bar whenever I want. I'm not used to being home..._babysitting."

Lilli felt like he'd slapped her. "I didn't know I was such a burden. I thought you were in love with me."

"I am, Lil. It's just, you can't really go out and do the things I'm used to doing."

"You mean, like Jenna."

"Yes, like Jenna. Jenna's an adult, with a job, who can go out and do what she wants."

"So, are you going to sleep with her?"

"I don't know."

The sting was unbearable. They were on Market Street now, with the throngs beginning to mill around and filter out to the bars. Hugh smiled and nodded to a girl in her twenties with long hair that was walking by them.

"Who was that? Do you know her?" Lilli asked, her mind and heart twirling.

"Uh, no, but I've seen her around."

"Around in the bars?"

"Yes, Lilli. In the bars, where people hang out."

"Do you think she's pretty?"

"What? Yeah, she's attractive."

"Prettier than me?"

"Lilli, why are you doing this?"

"I just want to know. You're out kissing girls while I'm home sleeping, saying hi to girls you've met in the bar while I'm standing right next to you, I just want to know if you think she's prettier than me."

"Fine, yes! She's prettier than you. Are you happy?"

Lilli couldn't respond. They had gotten to the door of their apartment. "Listen, I'm going out for a while," said Hugh. I'm going to meet Raymond at Smoochies."

"We just left him. What are you talking about?"

"I told him I'd meet him there in a little bit after I walked you home." Raymond was not twenty-one yet, either, but being tall with a beard, never had any problems drinking in the bars.

"So you're dumping me off to go drinking with Raymond?" she felt a little betrayed by Raymond. He had been her friend first.

"I'll be home in a little bit. Go upstairs, Lilli. Try to go to sleep."

"What time will you be home?"

"I don't know, Lilli. You're not my wife, and you're not my mother."

"I'm your girlfriend, aren't I?" she said, getting desperate.

"I'll be home when I get home."

"That's not fair. I really can't believe you're doing this."

Hugh sighed. "Fine, Lilli. I'll probably be home around midnight."

"Midnight?"

"Yes."

"Okay," she said, defeated. What choice did she have? Hugh gave her a quick hug and kissed her on top of her head. "I love you," she said, needing to hear him say it back.

"Love you, too, Lil."

♦ ♦ ♦

Midnight came and went with no sign of Hugh. Lilli waited a deadly ten, twenty, then thirty minutes, looking out the window down the street, then got dressed and went downstairs. She walked down the alley to Smoochies, hearing the sounds of laughter and loud music pouring out the open doors, sounds of exclusion. The bouncer sat on a stool by the open door. She stood on tiptoe trying to see over the fence onto the patio, where she thought she heard Hugh's deep voice.

"You looking for someone?" said the bouncer.

"My boyfriend... Hugh."

"You can go see if he's in there, just hurry up."

"Thanks," said Lilli and slipped past him into the dark bar. She tried not to feel self-conscious as eyes fell on her. She scanned around quickly, noticing Jenna bartending, and headed toward the patio. Hugh was out there, laughing with the girl from the street. "Hugh!" she couldn't help her accusatory tone.

"Lilli! What are you doing here?"

"You didn't come home! You said you'd be home by midnight." The girl was looking down her long nose at Lilli, as if she were an insect.

"What the fuck?" said Hugh. "So you're following me around now? This is ridiculous."

"You said you'd be home!"

"Go back home, Lilli," he said.

"No."

"You need to go home." Lilli shook her head, refusing. "You're going to get kicked out. You need to get out of here."

"I'm not leaving without you."

"Come on," he grabbed Lilli by the arm and began dragging her toward the door. "Sorry," he said to the girl. "I'll be right back." When they got out into the alley he dropped her arm. "How could you do this to me? You're embarrassing the fuck out of me."

"What, did I stop you from fucking that slut? I'm so sorry, Hugh. Sorry to keep you from putting your dick into someone else."

"You're acting like a child, Lilli. You need to get your shit together."

"I'm acting like a child! I'm trying to have a relationship with you and you're off trying to hook up with someone else!"

"I'm not trying to hook up with anyone! I'm just having a night out, something I haven't been able to do because I've been chained to your side!"

"I thought you loved me. I thought you loved being with me!"

"Not when you're being an immature little girl! I'm not your property. I have my own life, and I'm going to do my own thing. I can't be trapped by you."

"I'm not trying to trap you, I just don't want you fucking someone else!"

"You can't control me, Lilli! I'm going to sleep with whoever I want, and you can't do anything about it."

"I won't let you. I won't leave you alone. I'll stay out here all night. I won't let you go home with her."

"You are totally nuts. I'm going back inside." He turned to go back in the bar and Lilli grabbed at his sleeve. "Let me the fuck go!" he yelled, pulling away. A scuffle ensued, with Lilli grabbing after him and Hugh trying to disengage from her. He pulled away and when she lunged after him, his fist came smashing down on her nose. He was about to hit her again, but then someone was pulling him off of her. It was one of Hugh's old drummers, Sean. Coming upon them fighting in the alley, he had jumped in to Lilli's rescue.

"Shit, Lilli! You made me do that, you know!" Hugh boomed at her. It was louder than she'd ever heard his voice. "You need to go now! Leave me the fuck alone! Fucking crazy little bitch!" He turned to Sean. "Thanks, Man, sorry," he said to his buddy and went back into the bar.

"You okay, Lilli?" asked Sean, leaning down to hold her face between his hands and look more closely at her nose.

Lilli was totally stunned.

"Lil, you alright? I think it could be broken."

"It's fine," she said. "Thank you."

"That was fucked up. Are you sure you're okay?" Lilli nodded. "I'll talk to him," he said, and patting her on the shoulder, went into the bar after Hugh.

After he left, the sobs escaped. Lilli slid down the brick wall and sat with her face in her hands. Her nose was numb and throbbing, but actually felt good compared to the deep, wretched turmoil in her heart. The physical pain made sense. It was real, something that had a direct cause that she could trace. The deeper injury was a confusing and jumbled mess that tore through her chest. She felt completely hollow inside. Her whole world had turned upside down so quickly, and she had no idea how she had gotten there.

Chapter 12: Strawberries

Finn

Finn awoke on Sunday morning feeling out of sorts. She had been a little weirded out going over to Ella's. Being back in that old apartment, looking into the closet where Jake had slept before they became lovers, remembering all of the hiding places where she had stored her stash- it was a little unnerving. For the first time in a few months, she wanted to smoke... bad. For most of her recovery so far, the desire to use substances had been lifted. She felt like shit, she felt twitchy and nervous and emotionally all over the place, but she did not generally crave her old drugs anymore. The oldtimers at the meetings said the roller coaster would stop, and she held on to that. Usually, the roller coaster did not make her want to relapse, though. If anything, it made her want to put more distance between herself and her last binge. This was different, though, and she felt the urge to get high overtake her.

When she was in her old place, she could almost smell the weed again, although she knew she must have been imagining it. To think that Lilli was hanging out there was a little much, too. It was early, but she called Janie, who she knew would be up.

"Hi Babydoll," said the husky voice on the other end of the phone. Just that gave Finn comfort.

"Hi."

"What's the matter?"

"How do you know something's the matter?"

"C'mon Finn, I know you better than that. It's seven in the morning. If everything was fine, you'd wait until ten to call me."

"I love you, Janie."

"Me too, Sweetie, now what is it?"

"I went to my old apartment yesterday, to see Lilli. She was there with some friends. It just really freaked me out."

"What part bothered you?"

"Just seeing it again. I haven't been back there since I moved back to my mom's. Since Jake left."

"What else?"

"What do you mean what else?"

"What specifically bothered you?"

"I don't know, the smell. I mean, it must just be a sensory memory, but I remember the smell in there. Like bong water."

"Hmmmm," Janie said.

"Made me kind of want to come home and do

a bong hit. I kind of want to do one now."

"Of course you do."

"What do you mean?"

"Of course you want to smoke, you're an addict! There is nothing more natural in the world than an addict wanting to get high. You were in a place where you partied, where your whole life was about weed. That's called a 'trigger.' It's something that reminds you of the drug, a place, smell, certain people."

"People, places, and things," said Finn.

"Exactly."

"Yeah, but there was more. It was this girl, Ella. She said some things... about my dad, about my mom not telling me what the deal was with him."

"And?"

"And she's right, my mom really needs to tell me, but I don't know how to convince her. It's just bothering me even more now."

"So talk to your mom again."

"Yeah, I was planning on it. Lilli actually agreed to watch both of the kids today so that we could talk. Now I just have to get my mom to agree."

"Just tell her you're ready to hear it."

"Yeah, but am I? What if I really can't handle it? What if it's something really terrible?"

"You can handle it, Finn. It's to the point where the anxiety about it is worse than just knowing the truth."

"Yeah, you're probably right."

"So, do you have anything left in the house?"

"What do you mean?"

"Do you have any drugs left in the house?"

"No."

"Are you going to get high today?"

"No."

"Okay, then call me later."

"Okay."

"You can do this, Finnian. You've been through worse than this."

"Yeah, I have."

♦ ♦ ♦

Kairo was still sleeping. Finn called her mom.

"Oh, hi Honey. I was just going to call you.

"Why what's up?"

"Well... Ella Orlando called me last night."

"Ella called you?"

"Yes. She was worried about you. She told me you were really upset and that she felt like you really needed to know the truth about your dad. She said she thought it could jeopardize your sobriety."

"I can't believe she called you!" said Finn. That little minx!

"I don't want you to go back to drinking and getting high like you were, Finn. You've been doing so well. I think we should talk about it."

"Wow, okay."

"Sonja's coming over to watch the kids in a little bit, so we can talk." Sonja was the nice older lady who lived up the street. "Why don't you bring Kairo down when she gets here, then we can go up to your house to talk."

"Okay."

About an hour later, Evelyn was sitting on Finn's

couch, drinking tea. Finn fidgeted around for a while, then settled down on the other end of the couch facing her mother. "This feels really weird," she said.

"I know," said Evelyn and they both laughed nervously. "I don't even know where to start."

"How about the beginning?"

"Okay. You know, it's funny, but I've held on to it for so long, it just seems like a story now, not like something that really happened to me." She shifted on the couch. "Maybe I've kept it from being real by not talking about it, like as long as I didn't say it out loud it didn't really happen. It's been so hard to talk about to anyone, mostly because I feel like it was all my fault. I blamed myself for your dad dying. I should have known what kind of danger I was putting him in by loving him, but I didn't really know. I knew people were uncomfortable with it and that they were openly hostile, but I had no idea that they would ever hurt him. I had no idea anyone could ever do what they did to him. I survived and he didn't. I always thought I got off easy because I lived." She looked at Sadie. "I'm just going to say it, okay?" Sadie nodded. "They raped me, but they killed him. Shot him, actually, three times."

"Oh my god! Who?"

"The fucking cops. Three of them. I don't know how they found us. We were having a picnic out by the woods to get away from everybody. I remember I was wearing this dress with little red strawberries all over it. They started taunting him. He was resisting nonviolently, but when they grabbed me, he fought back. They dragged him into the woods and shot him. After I heard the shots, I completely left my body. I can't even say I was there for the rape. I thought they were going to kill me, too, but instead they threw me in the car and dumped me across the county line. They told me they'd kill me if I ever came back or if I told anyone.

"I got picked up by a truck driver who dropped me off in Asheville. He must have thought I was totally demented. I had lost my shoes, my dress was all torn and bloody. Some nuns, real nuns with habits and everything, found me sitting comatose in a park and brought me to a shelter. There was a woman there who was pregnant. Everyone said she was crazy because she talked to spirits out loud. She told me I had an angel inside of me and to take care of her. I thought she was crazy, too. I had no idea I was pregnant. It hadn't even occurred to me, I was so distraught. One of the older women at the shelter had to tell me she thought I was in "a family way" a few weeks later when I threw up two mornings in a row doing my chores.

"I had called my family to tell them I had met a girl in Alabama, and was going to spend the rest of the summer at her family's boat house on some lake near the shore. I could not even conceive of going home, but I didn't want them to come looking for me, either. The crazy lady came back several months later with a tiny little baby. She gave me a stained business card that said: "Help for Single Women Blessed with Child.' I called and the next day two women wearing handmade clothes and beads in their hair showed up and took me to the island.

"I was still in a total fog, but they were so incredibly nice to me. I barely spoke at all, and I never told them what had happened to me, but they were very respectful of my privacy. When you were born, I started crying, because right away I knew whose baby you were. At first the midwives thought I was crying because you were...black. But then they realized I was crying tears of joy. When you were born, it was like I woke up out of a nine month stupor. I had been sleepwalking, barely aware of my surroundings, just going where I was told to go and doing what I was told to do. When you were born, I came back to life.

"Over the years, I just focused on you. I just tried not to think about what happened to me and to your father. I made a habit of totally avoiding it. I figured I was lucky to even be alive."

"Holy crap, Mom. It doesn't sound like you got off easy."

"Of course you're right, but I never saw it like that. I just never wanted that to be your legacy. That's one of the reasons I didn't tell you. I never really wanted to face it myself, and you always seemed too young to have to carry the burden of what happened to me and to Finnian...to your father. So I kept it to myself."

"So now what?" asked Finn.

"What do you mean, now what?"

"I mean, now that it's out, now that you finally told me, can we get in touch with his family? I want to know who they are, and I think they should know who I am, that I exist."

"Finn," Evelyn started, "I don't really know if I'm ready for that. Think about this, I have held on to this for a quarter of a century. This is a big deal to me to be even telling you."

"But you loved him, and he loved you. Don't you think you at least owe it to his family to tell them what happened? I mean, they have gone 25 years without knowing what happened to their son. Maybe there's still some chance that those men could be prosecuted, if you told the truth about it."

"I really could not handle that. It's taken me this long to tell you, but I could not ever tell anyone else what they did to me."

"Well, maybe you could just tell them about what they did to him. I'm sure his parents would want to know, would want to know about me. Mom, maybe I have relatives that I could connect with. It's always been you and me, and yeah, Lilli too when she came along, but Lilli had some relatives from her dad's side. I never did."

"I do know his family's address," Evelyn admitted. "At least I know what it was 25 years ago. I have no idea if they are still there, if his parents are even still alive. He had a brother and sister, too. Maybe somebody is still living in that house."

"Let me write to them. I'll explain who I am and I'll keep you out of it."

"No, Finn. No, I really can't do that. I'll write it. I'm sorry, but I need to do it myself."

"Okay. Then when?"

"Shit, Finn. I'll do it soon, okay? I need to digest

this some more."

"Mom, the scary part is over. You told me and that's what you were so worried about."

"I'll do it, Finn. Just give me a little time, please. And please don't ask me about it again. I promise I'll do it when I'm ready, but please, can we just finally let it rest for now?"

Finn sighed. "Okay, mom, you're right, it's a big deal that you told me and I'm grateful. I really am." The two hugged and then Evelyn headed toward the door. "I'll bring Kairo up in a few. Can you watch Josey for a bit? I have to go to a Central American Support meeting."

"Of course, Mom, bring them both up."

"I don't know what I'd do without you, Finnie. Having you was the smartest thing I ever did." She walked back and gave Finn another long hug and kissed her on the head.

♦ ♦ ♦

After her mom came back from her meeting, they switched off again, and Finn headed into town. She had spoken to Janie to let her know what had happened, the story, and then had remembered that Lilli was expecting to watch the kids today. She would have figured out by then that Finn didn't need her help, but she decided to go tell her what she had found out. She needed to talk to someone else about it. Since Lilli did not have a phone, she decided to go check in with her. Knocking on the apartment door, she got no answer at first. When she was about to leave, Hugh opened the door.

"Hi Hugh," said Finn, avoiding his eyes. "Is Lilli here?"

"Uh- no, no, I think she might have gone to Ella's," said Hugh.

"Oh, okay, thanks. I'll head over there."

"Um, Finn, listen. We had a big fight last night, so she's probably really upset."

"Okay," she paused, thinking he was going to say something else.

"See you later, Finn," he said before closing the door.

What an odd bird. She had never really liked him. Even when they hung out back in the day, she found him really irritating. They had fooled around once when she was really drunk, and Finn had regretted it ever since. She still sold him pot after that, but tried not to have too much contact with him. She had a pretty low opinion of him, and it still made her very nervous that Lilli seemed so attached to him.

Ella looked surprised to find Finn at her door again.

"Hey, Ella. Is Lilli here?"

"Yeah, sure, Finn, come on in," she said.

This time, Finn knew she was not imagining the smell of pot wafting through the apartment. Lilli sat at the kitchen table with her friend, Sadie. She looked surprised when Finn walked in, and swept something under a magazine.

"Oh, hi, Finnie."

Finn could tell she was totally blasted. "Hi, Lilli. I just came to tell you that I didn't need you to watch the kids today."

"Yeah, when you didn't come this afternoon I figured it didn't work out with mom."

"No, it actually did work out. We got to talk. Sonja came to watch the kids."

"Really, wow!" said Ella. "Sit down, Finn, have a cup of tea. Tell us what happened," said Ella, starting to pour a cup.

"I don't know if I should stay," started Finn. Just then Lilli turned to her and Finn saw the bruise across her nose and swollen face. "What the fuck! Lilli, what happened to your face?"

"It's not what you think. Hugh and I had a fight last night, but it was an accident."

"That fucking bastard! I'm going to have his ass arrested!"

"No, Finn! It's not like that. I got in his face and he was just trying to push me away. It was an accident, really!"

Finn looked to Ella for confirmation, and Ella's purposefully neutral expression told her all she needed to know.

"I'm going to tell Mom. You can't live there anymore. You're sixteen years old! You shouldn't even be living on your own!"

"Stop it, Finn! Please just stop!" her voice broke. " I've had a really horrible day. Please just cut it out. I'm handling this in my own way."

"How, by getting wasted?"

Lilli looked up with her red eyes and just stared into Finn's, with defiance, but also deep sadness. Finn had a moment of compassion, remembering how not so very long ago, weed was the only thing that took away her own pain. "I'm sorry, Lil. It's your life. I know you probably don't need a lecture right now."

"No, I really don't."

"Okay, I'm sorry. We can talk about this some other time."

"Finn," interjected Ella, "I'm dying to know what happened with your mom. Sit down, have some tea. " She gestured to the cup of tea that she had put down at the empty space at the table.

"Honestly, Ella, it smells too much like pot in here. It's really a trigger for me. I shouldn't stay."

"Why don't we go in my room?" she suggested. "It should be pretty clear in there." Finn hesitated, but agreed.

They went in and sat around on the floor by the green couch, where Ella seated Finn. Finn felt a little bit like a queen with subjects around her. The air was, in fact, perfectly fine in Ella's bedroom.

"By the way, Ella. Thanks for calling my mom."

"You called our mom?" Lilli asked.

"Yeah, well. It was important," explained Ella.

"Well it worked. Nice strategy telling her you were worried about my sobriety. That's what did the trick."

"Honestly, Finn, I am worried about your sobriety."

"That's pretty funny, Ella. Sitting in a cloud of smoke, worrying about my recovery."

"Well, I reserve the right to contradict myself."

"Touché!"

"So what happened?" They all leaned in, waiting to hear Finn's story unfold.

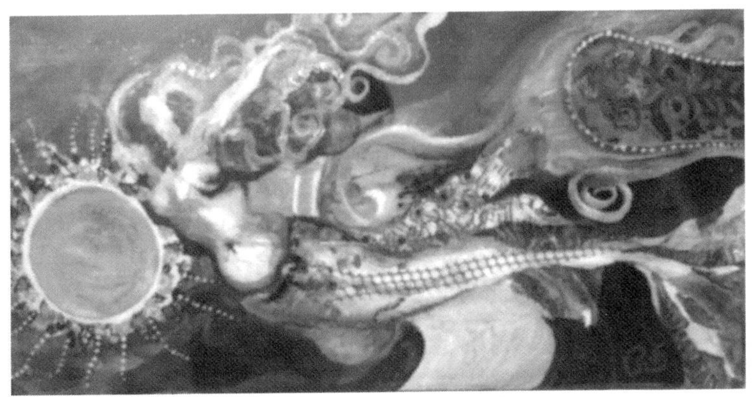

Part IV:

April 22-23, 1989

Chapter 13: Happy Family

Sadie

Sadie was picking out a birthday present. She had wandered into the expensive gift shop downtown to look for something nice for Kairo. He was turning four, and she really liked the little guy. After finding him a cute kit to build his own toy boat, she walked out into the beautiful spring air and headed toward her car. She had saved a lot of money since she quit drinking. She had even been able to buy a cheap used car from somebody she met at the meetings she had started to attend with Finn. As she started to cross the street to where her car was parked, she saw Raiche approaching on his bike.

"Hey, Sadie," he said with a smile. Raiche's smile was never joyful. It was the one you saw right before you got eaten.

"Oh, hi Raiche," said Sadie, still pulled in, even though she definitely knew better by now.

"What's up?" he said, straddling his bike.

"Oh, I'm just going out to Finn's house. It's Kairo's birthday, so I'm going to his birthday party," said Sadie.

"I heard you and Finn are dyking it."

"That's not true!"

"You know she's a dyke, right?"

"Who said that?"

"Everyone knows that. She used to rub pussies with that chick, Shara. And a bunch of other girls."

"So, who cares?"

"Well, she's probably after you, too," said Raiche, with a grin.

"I seriously doubt that."

"Just watch out, you're next. All the girls in Little Heart dyke-it eventually. They say it's in the water."

"Fuck you, Raiche."

"I did already, don't you remember?"

"No, actually, it's pretty hard to remember. It was so brief, and your dick was so small, it probably just slipped my mind."

Raiche cracked up, "Good one, Sadie! See you around." He jumped on the pedals and rolled up Chapel Street.

Sadie drove around the block and up behind Ella's apartment where she gave a few short honks. It took a few minutes, but Ella finally came out. She couldn't hide that she was pregnant anymore, as she had been doing for months. Her belly popped out under her big shirt and below the leather jacket that she still wore even though it was finally getting warm.

"Hi Sadie cakes!" said Ella as she jumped in to the front seat, still moving like she was not pregnant.

"Hi, Ella. You're looking kind of… big."

"Shit, I know."

"I just saw Raiche." She relayed the conversation to Ella.

"Glad you stuck up for yourself?"

"Yeah, but he always makes it seem like he wins in the end anyway."

"Yeah, he's a sly one."

"Is it true, though?" Sadie asked.

"What?"

"About Finn. Is she really a… lesbian?"

"Probably. So what?"

"I don't know. It's just, you don't think she'd try to hit on me, do you? I've been spending a lot of time with her, you know, at the meetings."

"So, what if she did?"

"Oh yeah, I forgot, you grew up around lesbians. That's probably no big deal to you."

"It is for you?"

"Yes! It is a big deal! It kind of freaks me out. I mean, what do they even do, together?"

"I'd imagine all the things you can do with a man, just without the dick."

"So you've never done it?"

"No. I have nothing against it. It's probably a curse, but I'm just attracted to men, unfortunately."

"Unfortunately?"

"Yeah well, life would be so much easier if I just

liked sleeping with women. It would be much less complicated," she said, and gestured with a sweeping arm toward her protruding stomach.

"Yeah, I guess."

"What about that chick you made out with at the Pub?

"What about it? I was really wasted," she said defensively.

"Yeah, but didn't you like it?"

Sadie had a flash of Lisa's hands running over her body and her soft lips. "I guess. It just really freaked me out."

"What did?"

"That I might be gay. I don't want to be gay."

"Because?"

"I have enough problems."

"Like?"

"Like, I'm trying to stay clean. I'm dealing with some crappy stuff that happened to me. I haven't had an easy life already, not that I didn't cause most of it."

"And being gay would mean…"

"That things would just be harder! That I'd be even more of an outcast. That people like Raiche would use me as a target forever."

"Sadie, in the big scope of the universe, Raiche is a tiny little nothing."

"Well, probably, but here in Little Heart, if he wants to, he can make your life pretty miserable. Remember the posters? And I don't think he was even trying."

"So let me ask you, have you ever enjoyed sex with men?"

"Um yeah, sure."

"Like with who?"

"Well there was this older guy I really liked, he worked at the college."

"And you liked fucking him?"

"Well, it wasn't great, but I really wanted to. I kept going back."

"Because you liked fucking him."

"I guess, I mean, I really liked him, so I really wanted to keep doing it with him."

"Because you wanted him to keep liking you."

"I guess."

"Liking someone and wanting them to like you is different than enjoying sex with them, Sadie."

"I guess so."

"So what happened with that guy?"

"He stopped calling, stopped returning my calls."

"And the others? Did you like sleeping with any of them?"

"Well, I liked them, except Hugh. That was kind of an accident."

"You slept with Hugh!"

"Yeah, I was drunk. It was one time. It never happened again. Please don't tell Lilli."

"Of course not. Was it good?"

"Of course not." They laughed.

Ella turned fully in her seat to face Sadie. "So, Sadie, do *you* think you're gay?"

"No! I'm not gay! Maybe I've just had some shitty experiences with men, but that doesn't make me a lesbian, Ella!"

"Maybe," said Ella, facing forward again. "Or

maybe you have had shitty experiences with men because you're a lesbian."

"Fuck you. If you weren't pregnant I'd drop you off on the side of the road."

"Thank god I like to fuck, or I'd be stranded by the side of the road by now!" The two giggled mercilessly for the rest of the ride to Finn's.

♦ ♦ ♦

Ella

Ella had not been to Evelyn's house since she was twelve and had first come back to Little Heart with her mother. It was nice to see the old house with ragtag lawn, little red barn, and pond, with spring flowers beginning to poke themselves up all around. Evelyn was an avid gardener. Ella remembered the last potluck she had been to at Evelyn's, late in the summer. All the kids had been playing outside, running under the hose. Ella had sat under a tree, reading Jane Austen. Being back there reminded her of her mom, and she missed her for the first time in a long time. She loved her mother, but had gotten so used to being on her own, living a life of lies where her mother still believed she was living with Aurora in Little Heart.

Evelyn came up to Ella, "Ella! Hi Honey," she said giving her a big hug being cautious of her belly. "It's so nice to see you! You're getting so big!" Ella hugged her back. "Thank you," Evelyn whispered in her ear when they embraced. It had been so many months, Ella didn't realize for a minute that she meant for calling to encourage her to talk to Finn about her dad. All the kids were running around and shrieking except for Josey, who hung on Evelyn's leg. Ella had met Kairo in town, but had not ever seen little Josephine before. Josey looked nothing like either Finn or Lilli. In fact, Ella observed, the three of them looked like they came from three different families.

"How's your mom?" Evelyn asked.

"Great! She's back on the island, you know," Evelyn nodded. Ella continued, "I don't get to talk to her often, but we write almost every week or so."

"Mary Ellen is a strong woman," said Evelyn. "You know, I never thought that when I gave her that card for the island when she was pregnant with you that she would end up staying there so long!"

"Yes, I think it's always felt more like home to her than anywhere else. It was hard when Catherine died, but I'm not surprised she ended up back there. It's still her home."

"Hi Sadie!" said Evelyn, moving on to give Sadie a hug. Sadie had been there a few times since she started going to meetings with Finn.

Evelyn went back to talking to the other mothers who had brought their kids to the party. Finn came over and gave each of them a hug and thanked them for coming. They went over to the picnic table and got some food and drinks, then sat on the new grass in the sun while the kids continued romping.

"Lilli's not coming?" inquired Sadie.

Finn snorted, "She knows about the party, but she never comes to these things. She's too wrapped up."

Sadie nodded. "Yeah, it seems like she's getting dragged through the wringer."

Finn did not seem very compassionate. "I told her Hugh was bad news. First of all, getting involved in a relationship with someone twelve years younger? What kind of creep does that?"

"A lot of creeps," noted Ella.

"Yeah, well, he's his own special kind," said Finn. "I don't feel sorry for her, she made her own decisions, and it's not like I haven't tried to help her."

"Do you think she'll ever get sober?" Sadie wondered.

"I doubt it. She really doesn't think she has a problem," said Finn. "Hey, did you call Janie? She said she had a suggestion for a new sponsor for you. I'm sorry it didn't work out with Pat. She can be flakey sometimes."

Ella got up and wandered back to the picnic table when Finn and Sadie started talking shop. She was happy for Sadie that she had made a connection to Finn and other people in the meetings, but she found it incredibly boring. She had stopped smoking herself when she realized she was pregnant, but all the recovery talk made her irritable. She had a hard time understanding what was so difficult about just making a decision not to do something and following through. People who were not totally in control of their lives made her impatient. But then, here she was, with a big belly she never intended having.

She had planned to just quietly flush out the growth in her uterus. She knew it would be easy to just take the herbs, eliminate the invading object, and go on with her life. When it came right down to it, though, floating in her bathtub, Adam's face popped into her mind. She was positive it was his baby, since when he had visited was the only time she had faltered and missed several days of taking the wild carrot seed. Adam was just so good, so really truly good. She couldn't do it to him. She had no intention of telling him about the baby, but when it came down to it, she couldn't just eliminate this piece of him.

Evelyn came over. "Honey, does your mom know about the baby?"

"No," said Ella.

"When are you going to tell her?"

"Soon."

"Are you keeping it?"

"Of course."

"Well, then, how are you not going to tell her?"

"To be honest, Evelyn, I haven't told her the truth about anything in years."

"Okay, but this is her grandchild," Evelyn said, her eyes sweeping out over the kids, landing on Kairo.

"She'll find out soon."

"What are your plans, Sweetie? Is the dad around?"

"No."

"You're going to stay in that apartment in town?"

"No."

Actually, it had occurred to Ella to move back into the attic, even without the tower. She would need someone to climb up the locker to open the attic door from the inside now that she was so big, but she figured she'd spend the last months of her pregnancy there and have the baby by herself. She felt confident she could deliver the baby and care for it in the attic for the first few months alone. She had begun collecting cloth diapers when she realized that this idea was pretty insane.

"Ella, it's none of my business," Evelyn said, "but, you really need to call your mother."

"You're right, Evelyn, it is none of your business."

"That may be true, but remember, it was never really any of your business to get involved between me and Finn, when I really needed to talk to her about her father." Ella nodded. "Sometimes women need to tell each other the truth." Evelyn looked her deeply in the eyes.

"Thank you, Evelyn. I'll think about that." She didn't want to tell Evelyn, but she had already decided to go back to the island. She'd been planning to leave for about a month.

"Good. And Ella..." she continued, "don't forget. Your mother is a midwife."

"Yes, I know," said Ella.

♦ ♦ ♦

Lilli:

Lilli had forgotten about the birthday party, but

had gotten a ride to her mother's to try to borrow money. The last few months had been a complete nightmare, and she was grasping at straws. Hugh had mostly left her, but she was still clinging to the idea that he would come back to her, although his cruelty had increased. He was blatantly sleeping with whoever he could, not coming home most nights, and they had gotten into a few more physical scuffles during times when she had followed him out to try to check up on him or prevent him from getting laid by any means necessary. She couldn't just let him go, though, even though she herself had gotten drunk and slept with other people a few times out of sheer desperation.

There had been some good times over the past several months. Usually Hugh would have some remorse, come back into Lilli's arms, complain about the woman he had slept with the night before, how she had grinded him too hard, or had puked on him. Lilli listened, grateful that he was telling her, grateful that he was back with her, that he recognized that she was the right one for him. They would have a reconciliation where Lilli was deeply hurt, but loving to him and just wanted any fragment of the normalcy that had begun their relationship.

After a few days of bliss and connectedness, where they were back tromping through puddles, Lilli supporting his musical creations from start to finish with some deeply loving moments, then something would happen to make her jealous again. He insisted that it was his right to look at other women, so she would notice him staring at one, wonder if that was the one he slept with last or if he only wanted to sleep with her. She wouldn't be able to help herself, so she would pester him, ask him questions, grill him, and then he would begin to back away, become hostile, and eventually go off drinking and hook up with someone else again.

Each time he moved further away. Lilli refused to let him go completely, but each incident was harsher and more purposely hurtful. The first few weeks after their relationship started falling apart, Lilli was in torturous pain. Every moment was excruciating. Then she noticed that when she smoked a lot, there was at least an hour or so when she was distracted enough to almost forget that she was so hurt. It came back when the weed wore off, but then the simple solution was to smoke again. This had worked for the first month or so, but over time, she was in constant distress that the weed couldn't touch.

Hugh had started staying with a friend of his. Natalie was a nice lady with a little boy. Hugh was clear telling Lilli he wanted to be with Natalie, but Natalie only seemed to want to be a friend to Hugh and help him out. Lilli thought she was very beautiful, with her long black hair and white skin. She was very nice to Lilli, helped her find Hugh when he went missing, and Lilli believed Natalie when she assured her she had no interest in him. Still, it was incredibly painful to know that he was staying there, yearning to be with Natalie, even if she had no intention of being with him.

One day she bumped into Raiche. He had moved out of the Trash House and into a room on the other side of Market Street toward the river. He invited her over and she went. She knew he was doing a lot of dope now. He still insisted that you couldn't get addicted if you only snorted. Lilli asked if she could have a line, and this time, Raiche gave it to her. In heroin, Lilli found a real solution. The high she got was so intense, so euphoric, that all of the pain completely disappeared. It wasn't the temporary numbing and hazy distraction she had gotten from pot, it was a deep and total reprieve.

She started buying bags from Raiche, ten or twenty dollars here or there. He introduced her to a friend, a nice dope addict, who lived in a room in an old mansion outside of town, who also hooked her up. Jerry was a little overweight, and had a loud raspy voice that kind of reminded her of Hugh. He was about Hugh's age, too. She started hanging out with him out of loneliness, and because he usually didn't charge her for the dope. She knew Jerry liked her, but his first love was heroin, so she didn't feel bad leading him on.

That Saturday, she was trying to get a ride to her mom's. Rent was due, Hugh was staying at Natalie's and had refused to kick in for their apartment, which he had mostly abandoned, and she had no money even to eat. Jerry had to go to pick something up in Kingsdale anyway, so he told her he'd drop her off at her mother's and pick her up on his way back through. She and Jerry had smoked a joint in the car and she was totally baked. As soon as she walked down the driveway, she remembered the party and realized going there was a big mistake. She saw the balloons and heard all the laughing kids, and the clincher was seeing Finn there, hanging out with Sadie and Ella like old pals.

"Honey! You made it," said her mom, running over to hug and kiss her.

"Yeah, sorry, I don't have a present for Kairo. I'm totally broke."

"You're here! That's all that matters."

Kairo ran up to her and gave her a big hug and then Josey followed suit, both of them hanging on to her like little monkeys. "Hey you guys!"

"Lilli, Lilli, Lil, Lil, Lilli!" yelled Kairo. "Did you bring me a present, Aunt Lilli?"

"Sorry, Kairo, I'm going to make something for you, but I didn't bring it with me this time. I'll give it to you next time, okay?"

"Okay!" They gave her a few more squeezes and ran back to their friends.

She got a plate of food and went over and sat on the grass next to Sadie, Finn, and Ella, whose belly looked enormous to Lilli. "Hi guys." Finn just stared at her. "What?"

"You are totally high. I can't believe you came to my kid's birthday party totally high." Finn got up and walked away.

"Shit, what is her problem?" asked Lilli as her sister walked away. She looked to the other two, hoping to see some kind of disbelief at Finn's obviously rude behavior, but they just looked intently at her.

"How're you doing, Lilli?" asked Ella.

"Pretty crappy. I'm about to get kicked out of

my apartment, I have no money, no food. Hugh is pretty much living with Natalie. And… my sister hates me, so I guess not really that great."

"How did you get here?"

"I got a ride from Jerry- do you know him? He lives out at the Maddentown Mansion, you know, the Mad Hatter House?"

"Yeah, I know Jerry. He's kind of a dope fiend," said Ella.

"Nah, he's really nice. He's helped me a lot, given me some rides, bought me dinner a few times. He's not a bad guy."

"No, but he's a dope fiend," said Ella.

"Yeah, well, everybody can't be perfect."

It was time for cake and presents, and Lilli welcomed the distraction. As soon as she could pull her mother aside, she told her about her dilemma. "I'm gonna get kicked out, Mom. The social security money doesn't cover everything, and I had to use it all to pay last month's rent, since Hugh isn't helping anymore."

"Why don't you come back here, Lilli? We have plenty of room. Josey would love to have you here again. We all would."

"I can't do that, Mom. I need to be near Town. I need to be with my friends."

"I know, but what's your plan? If you can't afford your place by yourself, what are you going to do?"

"I don't know. I'm probably going to move. There are rooms at my friend's place in Maddentown. They're a lot cheaper than the ones right on Market Street. Rent is due next week, I'll probably just skip out on the place I live now and rent a room in Maddentown. I'd need money for security, though, and my check doesn't come until next week. And I'm totally broke. I don't have anything to eat in the house at all. My friends have been helping to feed me, but I hate to mooch off of them all the time."

"I'll get my checkbook," said Evelyn.

As soon as she could break away, Lilli went up to wait for Jerry at the top of the driveway. "Bye, guys! Bye Kairo, love you, kiddo! Happy Birthday!" Lilli had a blank check in her pocket and a twenty dollar bill that Evelyn had given her to buy some groceries.

♦ ♦ ♦

Finn:

Finn was indignant. "Did you really give her money?" she asked Evelyn, as they were cleaning up after the party.

"She's my daughter, Finn. What am I supposed to do? She's in a really hard place."

"Mom! She's just going to use it to get high!"

"No, I didn't give her cash. I gave her a blank check to write out to the new landlord for security on her new place. She has to move out of her apartment on Market Street because Hugh is moving out."

"You gave her a blank check?"

"Yes. She doesn't know the new landlord's name or exactly how much the security will be."

"You have to be kidding me!"

"Finnie, sometimes you have to just trust that your children are going to do the right thing. Lilli is a good person. She's really struggling. She needs help."

"Yeah, Mom, but sometimes helping doesn't help."

"When Kairo's older, you'll understand."

Kairo had a great day, and was pretty tuckered out. Finn let him sit and watch a video. She didn't do that as much as she used to anymore. Setting up the kids with videos used to be her way to sleep in when she had a hangover, but she used them a lot more sparingly now. She was a little wiped out, too, though. She was coming up on a year clean, but Finn still had trouble with some of the most basic parts of just living a normal life. Something as simple as a kid's birthday party seemed to be a very big ordeal and took a lot out of her.

She had to go to Janie's anniversary that night, though. Janie was celebrating eight years sober and Finn was supposed to speak for her. She had never told her story at a meeting before, and this was probably going to be a big celebration with a lot of people there. Just thinking about it made her feel nauseous. She wondered if she should make some valerian root tea, but was worried that she might get too drowsy. She was about to pick up the phone to call Janie to try to get some pointers on how to relax so that she could get through the anniversary, when she heard a car pull down the driveway.

She went to the front window. Two black men in

suits were getting out of the vehicle. The older one was graying and walked with a cane, and the younger one held some papers in his hand. Great. Jehovahs. Just what she needed right now. As she watched them coming up the walkway, she rehearsed what she had found was the fastest way to get rid of them. Usually, she just told them that she was a lesbian witch and that she worshipped trees and rocks. That generally had them hightailing it out of there pretty quickly.

When they got up the steps and knocked, she opened the door and prepared to proclaim her pagan identity, but before she could, the older man said, "Hello, there. Are you Finnian Endicott?"

Finn took a step back. "Yes. Who are you?"

The older man sighed deeply. Looking directly into her eyes, he said, "I'm Finnian Endicott."

Chapter 14: *Finnian Endicott*

He really wasn't that old, Finn found out as they sat in Evelyn's living room, only 50, about seven years older than her mom. He had just had a pretty rough life. After he was left for dead, he had spent almost a year in the hospital recovering from the bullet wounds. He had been transferred to a state hospital, thankfully, away from the perpetrators. Multiple surgeries were needed to save his groin and leg, where he had been shot twice, and for the shot in his chest, which had punctured a lung. Afterward, he was sent to a long-term rehabilitation clinic in Georgia, where an aunt and uncle and many cousins kept tabs on him through the recovery process, sending back word to his parents, who had stayed in Alabama.

He never knew what became of Evelyn, thinking that they had probably killed her, and his few contacts in the movement up North said she never came back from her trip. Finnian stayed in Georgia with his extended family, and five years later, married and had a son. The boy was now the young man who accompanied him, Everest, that everyone called "Ever." Ever was twenty, in college in Georgia planning to go into law. Several years before, Ever's mother had died of stomach cancer.

Evelyn sat on the couch next to Finnian, holding his hand and gazing at him. She explained to Finn that she had sent the letter she had promised to send to his parents, letting them know they had a granddaughter and where they could get in touch with her. She had not heard back, and after several months, she had assumed the letter had not reached them, that they had moved or had died. Really, they had passed the letter on right away, and Finnian had been waiting until Ever could drive him up, since he had trouble driving long distances.

Finn sat staring at her father, totally speechless. Having never even seen a picture of him, it was totally surreal to recognize aspects of his features that were present in her own face and body. And a brother! She looked shyly at Ever, realizing she was the big sister to a full-grown man that she had never met before. The four of them sat with the kids playing in the next room, talking haltingly and trying to catch up on a quarter of a century. Kairo was introduced to his grandfather, and took it with the same nonchalance as if he had been told he was delivering the mail.

Pretty soon, it was time to go to the meeting. Finn had almost forgotten, but when it started getting dark, she realized that she still needed to speak for Janie. Her parents, so strange to think that she actually had *parents*, insisted on coming with her. They would keep the kids quiet in the back, and then they could all go out to dinner afterward. She was nervous enough already about speaking in public about her decline into alcoholism, but didn't really see how she could say no.

The room was packed with about a hundred people present. Finn was put up in front with a podium. She felt like rubber and trembled right down into her fingertips, but made herself open her mouth and say, "Hello, my name is Finnian, and I'm an alcoholic."

After the first few sentences, it came more naturally, and Finn described how she had begun, had always felt different and had tried to blend in by finding her place in the twisted subculture of Little Heart. She got to the end, painting a picture of her deterioration, her alienation, and the seemingly divine intervention that had carried her into a meeting one day when all she really wanted to do was die. She spoke about the gifts of the past year, going back to school, being more present as a parent, and starting to repair her life. She explained how having the courage to face her life had even led to her being reunited with her father. She thanked Janie publically for all she had done to help her, and congratulated her on her anniversary.

Finn finished and looked up, scanning the back of the room for where her family had been, but they weren't there. She looked by the door, and saw her mother, speaking urgently to... *Hugh*. As gracefully as she could, she backed away from the podium as people clapped and the chair person took over the microphone. She headed toward the back of the room to see what the commotion was about.

"What's going on?" she asked her mother, who looked at her with wild, terrified eyes.

"It's Lilli," she said.

Chapter 15: *Lillian Vaughn*

Lilli waited at the top of her mother's driveway. Shortly, Jerry pulled up in his beat up old white Cadillac. When she got in the car, he gave her a big sweaty kiss. Were they a couple now? She wasn't sure how that happened. "Hey, what'd you get?" he asked.

"She just gave me twenty. I got a check for rent, though, so I can move out of my apartment. There's still that room on the first floor at your place, right?"

"Sure, yeah it's open. The old alchy geezer there went into a nursing home. Smells like piss, though, even though they cleaned it."

"That's gross. I don't want to live in a room that smells like piss."

"That's okay, you can stay with me until another room opens up."

Lilli felt her world closing in around her. "I guess

we'll see what happens. Maybe I can find another place in town."

"I gotta make a stop at Raiche's. He picked up a bundle and I told him I'd split it with him.

"Okay."

Lilli followed Jerry up to Raiche's apartment. She felt a surge of disgust as he wheezed up the stairs in front of her. At Raiche's kitchen table she just kind of tuned out, looking out the window while the men talked. She was hoping to buy a bag of her own from Raiche so she wouldn't be indebted to Jerry, but she figured she'd wait until they were done with their transaction.

"What do you think, Lilli?"

"What?"

"Raiche has a brick, he said he'd sell us half for $200. That's like getting five bags for free."

"If you want." She was not sure how many bags were in a brick.

"I only have $100, so you want to split it with me?"

"I only have $20."

"But you have that check from your mom. It's blank, right?"

"That's for rent."

"Yeah, but there's not even a room available yet, except the smelly one that you don't want. Look, you can stay with me. Tell your mom you needed to chip in on a temporary place until a room opens up. She'll understand."

Lilli squirmed and looked at Raiche. "It's a good deal," he said. "Just make it out to 'cash.'"

"Okay," she said, taking the check from her

pocket.

Back at the Mansion, Jerry suggested they stop by to buy a bag of weed from the hippies on the first floor with Lilli's remaining $20. She had met the couple selling weed before, had seen them in town with their baby driving around in their painted-up VW bus. They were living together with their toddler in a room with big windows. They seemed really sweet, and Lilli felt a pang of jealousy over the tiny place in the world they had carved out for themselves. Maybe living in the house with them wouldn't be so bad. They could be friends.

Jerry rolled a joint and they smoked before he started opening the bags of dope, so many, Lilli couldn't imagine what they would do with them all.

"Do you want to skin pop?" Jerry asked. "I have a new needle. You can use it first."

Lilli hesitated. She had only snorted heroin up to that point. Jerry took her silence to be ascent and began prepping. He told her to roll over onto her stomach and then pulled down the top of her skirt and tights to shoot the heroin into the top of her ass. It really didn't hurt, especially after the drug quickly entered her system. She was in heaven! It was a much more intense high than she had ever gotten from the dope before, and she really, really liked it.

She was vaguely aware of Jerry shooting up into his hand, and then he was on the bed, kissing her and taking her clothes off. Then they were fucking, with Jerry's bulging sweaty body feeling like a massive weight, but Lilli was so high, her repulsion was far, far away. Time was pretty muddled, but Jerry seemed to get limp and distracted from being so high, and then he was cooking up more on a spoon. Lilli was not feeling like she needed more, but didn't want to stop feeling good, either. She let him shoot into her other butt cheek.

She was in reverie again. Nothing mattered. Hugh didn't matter, being stuck here with this nice, but kind of nauseating dope addict didn't matter, her mother's money didn't matter. She had found the solution to all of her pain, all of her problems. She had found nirvana on earth.

She didn't even realize she was having trouble breathing until she saw Jerry's big face over her, asking her if she was okay. She tried to answer, but she didn't really care enough to and didn't seem to have enough breath.

In moments, everything went black.

Chapter 16: *Ella Orlando*

Ella stood in front of the field across from the tower, or where the tower used to be. The workers had removed the tarp on the roof and replaced it with metal sheeting, nailed over the gaping hole. There was talk about rebuilding the tower eventually, but nobody seemed to know where the $500,000 they said it would take to replace it would come from. Ella doubted it would ever happen. The sight of the missing structure was less painful now than it had been in November when it happened. Standing across the field with her rounded belly, it seemed like the whole universe had probably just come into balance as it always does; one thing removed, one thing added. Somehow, the tower was inside of her now.

Kelpie ran in circles around Ella, as always, but seemed to sense from her mistress that something was different this time. Ella did not know when she would be back here again. Walking back to the apartment, the gravel and cigarette butts on the ground appeared in sharp focus. She rounded the corner and saw Cooper sitting on her step, reading the paper, already guzzling his forty.

"I figured you'd be right back," said Coop, patting Kelpie who nipped around his hand, looking for the elusive bats.

They went inside, and Ella put the coffee on while Cooper settled in with his pen and crossword. He scratched quickly for a while, then looked up at Ella. "So, what are you going to do?" he asked her.

"What do you mean?"

"About the baby." He had never mentioned her pregnancy before, which had become more apparent in the last month or so.

"I'm having the baby, obviously," said Ella, indicating her round stomach.

"I know, but are you keeping it?"

"Of course," said Ella.

"Who's the father?"

"Not you."

"I know, I mean, I figured you would have mentioned it to me."

"Yes, I would have."

"Okay, well, do you need anything?"

"Like what?"

"I don't know, a crib, diapers, someone to claim paternity?"

"No, Coop. I'm good. But thanks for asking." Cooper nodded and went back to his puzzle. "Listen, Cooper, I won't be here tomorrow." He looked up, questioning. "I'm going home. I'm going to my mom's place."

"You're taking Kelpie?" Cooper looked sadly down at the little brown dog, whose head was nestled on his knee, and petted her lovingly.

"No, actually Sadie's going to be here to take care of her."

"Sadie?"

"Yeah, she's taking over my lease. She's going to keep Kelpie until I can come and get her in a few months. She's moving in tonight. Do you think you can come and walk her sometimes?"

"Who, Sadie?"

"Ha ha. I'm serious, Coop. Can you take Kelpie out sometimes? You could probably still come over in the mornings."

"I will, for now. I probably won't be here for long, though."

"Really? Where are you going?"

"I'm moving back up North. No Heart, New York can kiss my ass."

"Okay, well here's my address," she handed him a slip of paper.

"I'll send the baby tapes. Good music, and not that lullaby bullshit, either."

"Okay, Coop. That'd be nice."

After he left, Ella continued cleaning up. She was leaving most of what she had accumulated since coming back to Little Heart to Sadie. Sadie didn't really have anything, so all the pots and pans, furniture, and general household things would come in handy for her. Ella really just packed a few books and any of the clothes that still fit her into a big black duffel bag. She was busy packing away her old bongs, pipes, and rolling trays into a box, since neither she nor Sadie would be needing them, when there was a knock at the door.

She was surprised to see Seth, the snaggletooth drug dealer turned hopeless romantic. She hadn't seen him in months.

"Can I come in?" he asked.

"Sure."

He followed her into the kitchen. She leaned against the counter and waited for what he could possibly have to say. "I heard you were knocked up," he said, cutting to the chase.

"Classy," she replied.

"I know it's mine, Ella," he said.

"Actually, Seth, it's not yours. I was using birth control when we were sleeping together."

"You can say that, but I know it's mine."

"Well then you're sorely mistaken."

"C'mon, Ella. I'm right here and I'll stay right here if you want, even if it's not mine."

"Thank you, Seth, but that's not necessary."

"You'd think you'd be thrilled to have someone willing to take responsibility for your baby."

"What are you talking about? *I'm* taking responsibility for my baby."

"But don't you want the baby to have a father?"

"Not particularly," she admitted.

"Okay well, I'm not going to offer again. Don't come to me when he's five asking me to buy him sneakers."

"Why on earth would you ever assume it's a

boy?"

Seth just shook his head. "You're fucked." He turned to leave.

"Thank you, and Seth?"

"What?" he turned around.

"Here," she shoved the box of paraphernalia at him. "Can you give these away to poor children who can't afford bongs?"

He looked in the box, then looked at her. "Fucked," he repeated, and then went out the door carrying the box.

Ella continued cleaning up and finished packing her duffel bag. Her only loose end was Zep. She had written to him, admitting that she was pregnant a few months back, but he had never responded. She knew she had betrayed him by giving in to her biology, not rising above her primal instinct to procreate, as he would see it. At around ten, Sadie came to the door.

"I thought we weren't going to do the goodbye thing?" Ella said.

"We weren't but..."

"But you missed me so much already?" Ella smiled.

"No, well, yeah, but that's not why I'm here. I wanted to tell you about Lilli... she overdosed last night."

"Shit. Is she okay?"

"Yeah, she is now. They took her to St. Sebastian. She barely made it. Her breathing had stopped."

"Holy shit."

"Yeah, Finn's a wreck. She's been at the hospital all night."

"That dope fiend Jerry, he's bad news."

"Actually, she got it from Raiche."

"Oh, wow."

"Yeah."

"So, what's going to happen?"

"Lilli's supposed to go to rehab. The social worker was talking about sending her to this halfway house for women afterward. She could be there for up to a year. I don't think they're pressing charges on Raiche or anything."

"So Raiche gets away with it, again."

"Like always," said Sadie.

"Well, maybe not," said Ella. Sadie looked at her, confused. "Don't you believe in karma, Sadie?"

"Um, I guess."

"Can you imagine the karmic load Raiche has to bear?"

"So what, bad things will happen to him? He'll get hit by a truck?"

"Maybe, or maybe not. Maybe instead he'll live to a nice, ripe old age. The worst karma for Raiche might be living out his awful, miserable life for decades and decades, in squalor, alone, with nobody loving him forever."

That rang true for Sadie. "That sounds worse than the truck."

"Oh, it will be," said Ella.

♦ ♦ ♦

Saying goodbye to Kelpie was the worst. She

spent almost an hour with her on her ever-shrinking lap, the dog's chin tucked under her own neck. She had promised herself she would never be separated from her dog again. "Sadie's going to be back soon," she told Kelpie, imagining the confusion her pup was going to experience when Sadie showed up that night and Ella did not return.

She took a last look around, but there was little that she even cared about. She had sold her few remaining bags of weed the night before. The last thing she did was go to her closet and take out a paper bag she had stashed in between the futon and the wall that held approximately $12,000. She had saved almost all of her profit since returning to Little Heart. She put it in the bottom of her duffel and lugged the bag out of the apartment and up the street. It was only a few blocks to the bus station. Turning the corner by the bookstore, she ran into Hugh. He was carrying a cup of coffee.

"Oh, hi Ella. Where you going?"

"I'm heading out of town for a while."

"Did you hear what happened to Lilli?"

"Yeah, Sadie told me."

"That was really fucked up. Those hippies dropped her off on the street. I think she was overdosing out at Jerry's place and everybody there freaked out. Nobody wanted to get arrested, so they dumped her off here."

"That is fucked up."

"Nobody knew what she had taken. Ditto came to get me, and then I called the ambulance."

"How thoughtful."

"Yeah, she's gonna be okay, though. I talked to Finn this morning and they're going to send her away for a long time, to rehab."

"So, you're off the hook."

"It's not like that, Ella. I really cared about Lilli, but things changed between us. She just couldn't adapt to it."

"Silly girl, she couldn't adapt to being loved and then dropped cold. Yeah, I see how that could be really inconvenient for you."

"You don't get it, Ella. Lilli's really immature."

"She's fucking sixteen, Hugh. What did you expect?"

"Yeah, but I never promised her anything. She made all these demands on me."

"But she's sixteen."

"She just drove me crazy, following me around, 'I love you, Hugh,' 'I love you, Hughey,' it was like being chased by an annoying doll."

"Yeah, I see what you mean. It would have been much more useful if she had just stayed a fuck-me toy. "

"Forget it, you don't understand. I really loved her in the beginning."

"Too bad you realized that... she's sixteen!"

"Fuck you, Ella. Have a nice life." He started to walk away.

"And I wish you a nice, long life, too, Hugh." She said to his back. She turned and continued up the street, wondering what karma had in store for him.

At the bus station Ella sat on the wooden bench outside in the bright sunlight, facing down Market Street, the brick buildings like a movie façade. The mountains floated in the distance like a backdrop. So many people came to Little Heart and stayed to see that view every day. The picturesque beauty of the river and the fields, the peaceful farms and rocky vista, it all gave the impression that life here would be idyllic and wholesome. People came to go to college and never left. It was a nice place to settle down after a long bender on Market Street.

A pickup truck pulled up in front of the bus station. Ella did not pay attention until she realized that the driver was looking at her and leaning over to roll down the passenger side window to talk to her. It took her a few seconds to realize that it was *Adam*. She stood up and walked over to the truck.

"What's a nice girl like you doing in a place like this?"

"Waiting for a guy like you to come along and give me a line like that." They both laughed.

"Can you get in, Ella?"

She went back and fetched her bag, but suddenly Adam was out of the truck and taking the duffel from her hands, tossing it in the back of the truck. She got in the front seat, suddenly aware and self-conscious of her large abdomen. She looked over and realized that Adam was looking at her, but that he did not seem at all surprised by her state.

"I'm not here to ask you to marry me again, Ella."

"But how did you…" recognition flashed across her face. "Sadie," she finished.

"Sadie," he acknowledged.

"So then why are you…?"

"I'm here to take you home…to the island. I sent your mother a letter. She called me a few days ago. The Council met, and they decided that I can stay there, too, until the baby comes."

"So my mother knows I'm pregnant?"

"Yes."

"And they agreed to let you stay there?"

"Yes."

"And you want to, you want to go there… with me?"

"Yes. I want to be there with you for the birth of our child."

"And then?"

"And then we'll figure it out."

"*We* will?"

"Yes. I don't know if you realize this, Ella, but the baby is only part of the reason that I'm here."

"What's the other part?"

"I love you."

Ella expected these words to make her cringe, but they didn't. There was no fantasy in them, no projection, no *elpis*.

The bus was pulling in behind Adam's truck and let out two short honks. Adam began driving. Ella realized he had a map and had already marked out the directions to the island. He got to the corner and put his blinker on.

"Wait!" Ella exclaimed.

Adam looked startled. "What?" he asked.

"We need to go get my dog."

Epilogue.

April 2, 1989

Dear Adam:

You don't know me, but I'm a friend of Ella's. Or at least, I'm her friend now. I don't know if I'll still be her friend once she finds out that I'm writing you this letter. I need to inform you that Ella is pregnant. I know that this might be hard for you to believe, especially because of how you and Ella first met and how she lied to you about being pregnant before. I can guarantee that she really is about seven months pregnant, and if you do the math, you will find that it is yours.

I am writing to you because I know she never would. She's too proud. I have reason to believe that she would want you to know, though. I can't go into details, but I believe that she was in love with you. After you found out about her scam, I think she felt like you would never trust her again, so she didn't even try to repair it. In some ways, I think Ella did not believe she deserved to repair it. I know that she regrets hurting you, though.

I've gotten to know Ella pretty well over this past winter, and one thing I can say about her is that as independent as she is, there is something very lonely about her. She only lets a few people into her inner world, and she definitely let you in. She told me that you were the only man who has ever seen her for who she truly is.

I know it might be hard to forgive her for what she did to you, but remember that when she first did it, she barely knew you. I know you know a little bit about how Ella grew up, so I'm sure you can understand that she thinks a little differently than other people.

Ella is going back home to have the baby. She is planning to take the bus out of Little Heart at 2:00 pm on Sunday, April 23rd. I am telling you this on the off chance that you would actually like to see her before she goes.

In case you do not want to see her in person, I am attaching her mother's address on the island so you can write to her there. I think Ella would like that. You never know, maybe it will all work out.

Sincerely,

Sadie Lane

Scribbled on the back of a bus ticket:

Sadie- You little devil!

Adam is here to take me home to the island. We're taking Kelpie.

I should probably kill you, but instead I'm going to name my baby Sadie Lane Orlando.

Come visit us!

Love,

Ella

5/29/89

Dear Finn:

Brookside is actually not such a bad place. The girls here are pretty tough, and there's a lot of petty shit, but everyone really supports one another.

We're in group together all morning, then lunch and chores, then we meet with our therapists, case managers, and have other appointments in the afternoon. A lot of the girls are in legal trouble, so they have to go to court. There are two girls who are pregnant. We have to go to meetings in the community every night.

I miss Hugh. I know you probably think that's stupid, but I do. My therapist says he's an "attachment object" and that I fixated on him because my dad died and I left home too early. I think that's ridiculous. I just love him. He's the first one who really loved me and stayed with me. I just want it to go back to the way it was in the beginning when he loved me. I haven't heard from him, even though I've written him letters.

You know, Finn, I really don't think drugs were my problem, even after the overdose. I just wanted to stop being in pain. My heart was broken. A lot of the residents here talk about how they were obsessed with getting high and how it took over everything and how they hurt everyone in their lives because they chose drugs over them. I don't feel that way. I just wanted Hugh. If I had him, I could care less about the drugs. I'll admit there were some times when it got out of control, but I really think I could have stopped at any time if Hugh had been there with me.

If anything, maybe I'm a love addict. I don't know what the treatment is for that, but this is probably not it. I don't feel like I belong here, but here I am. I know that even if Mom doesn't put that PINS petition on me if I leave, the counselors here will. I guess I gave up my rights when I overdosed. Technically, I'm still a minor and that means that everyone else gets to decide what's best for me regardless of whether I agree.

They say I'm clinically depressed and want to give me drugs for it. Drugs! Hypocrites! They say I was self-medicating, and who knows, maybe they're right about that.

Anyway, I'm sure you're gloating and thinking that you told me so. Everyone here tells me to look at the evidence of where my "addiction" took me, to the brink of death. I don't really believe that, but I have a feeling they won't let me leave until I admit I have a problem. I do have problems, but I still won't call myself an addict. Even in group when everyone says, "I'm so and so, and I'm an addict," I still just say: "I'm Lilli."

This has been kind of good for me, though. I'm getting my equivalency diploma, meeting with counselors, trying to figure out what to do with the rest of my life. I took a career assessment the other day and it said I should go into social work. Can you imagine? Me, a social worker? Social case, maybe. I miss Little Heart, but it probably won't kill me to stay here and get fed regularly, take care of some things.

Thanks for the letter. I'm glad you found your dad. He sounds really great. Oh, and congratulations on your anniversary. One whole year sober. That's very cool.

Your Sister,

Lilli

June 18, 1989

Dear Sadie:

I was really surprised to get your letter. I would never have thought that when you went to visit Ella you could end up staying. A midwife! That is so cool. I got chills all over when I read about how the moment you saw little baby Sadie being born you knew what you were going to do with your life.

I wish I knew what I wanted to do with my life. I know I want to stay sober, but that's about it. I love school, but every new class I take confuses me even more. I take an English literature class and I want to become a writer, I take an earth science class, and suddenly I want to be a geologist. I'm taking a Baroque Art class for summer session, and now I want to be an art historian. The world is just so full of possibilities and I'm interested in everything. It's pretty overwhelming. I guess this is what they would call a "luxury problem," because a year ago my options were drug dealer or waitress.

I've been writing to my dad in Georgia. My mom and Kairo and I are going to go visit him in August after summer session ends and before school begins in the fall. Kairo needs to start getting to know his grandpa, and I want to meet more of my family. Honestly, I think my mom is still in love with my dad. All the drama going on with Lilli overdosing kind of overshadowed whatever they were rekindling, but it was very hard for them to say goodbye when he had to go back.

Maybe on the way back from Georgia we'll swing by the island. Even though I was born there, I've never been back. I think my mom would want to visit, too. It would be really cool to see how a society of all women functions (see, I even want to be an anthropologist, or a sociologist, or maybe just a feminist!). Which reminds me, that's pretty amazing that they decided to let Adam stay there for the birth. I guess Ella and her mother are kind of like island royalty, and the rules get bent for royalty. Are they really going back to Iowa? I have such a hard time picturing Ella on a farm. Or maybe that's exactly where she belongs.

Lilli is still at Brookside. She writes to me pretty much every week telling me how terrible it is that they're making her stay there and then telling me how great the friendships are and how well she is doing. She got her G.E.D., and she's volunteering at a food pantry. I'm so grateful that she's there, even if she doesn't get it right now. Her life has been saved and hopefully she'll see that someday. I don't know what life has in store for her, but I guess that's none of my business.

Who knows? The longer I stay clean the more I realize I just don't know anything. I don't know what's right for other people and I certainly don't know what's right for me. Janie says it's healthy to develop tolerance for ambiguity. She says it leaves you open for the Universe's will for you. I am still skeptical about the whole god thing, but I do know that my life has changed drastically since I got sober. Maybe there's a reason for that. Maybe there's a plan for me and maybe I don't need to know what it is right now.

Well, I'm glad at least that the Universe has revealed its plan for you! I'm really happy for you, Sadie. I will miss you, though. I'll let you know when I'm coming to visit. Say hello to Ella for me, and give Baby Sadie a kiss.

Love Always,

Finn

Nikki Pison, PhD, LMHC

Nikki Pison is an artist, writer, and mental health professional living in upstate New York. She holds a PhD in psychology from Capella University, a Master of Arts in psychology from SUNY New Paltz, and a Bachelor of Arts in psychology from Vassar College. Dr. Pison is a New York State Licensed Mental Health Counselor with a background in research, substance abuse treatment, and psychotherapy, specializing in cognitive behavioral interventions. She regularly writes and presents on numerous mental health topics. *The Cusp of Sad* is her first work of fiction.